RED ZONE

RED ZONE

Tiki Barber and Ronde Barber
with Paul Mantell

A Paula Wiseman Book
Simon & Schuster Books for Young Readers
New York London Toronto Sydney

For AJ and Chason—T. B.

For my three roses—R. B.

SIMON & SCHUSTER BOOKS FOR YOUNG READERS
An imprint of Simon & Schuster Children's Publishing Division
1230 Avenue of the Americas, New York, New York 10020
This book is a work of fiction. Any references to historical events, real people, or real locales are used
fictitiously. Other names, characters, places, and incidents are products of the author's imagination,
and any resemblance to actual events or locales or persons, living or dead, is entirely coincidental.
SIMON & SCHUSTER BOOKS FOR YOUNG READERS is a trademark of Simon & Schuster, Inc.
For information about special discounts for bulk purchases, please contact Simon & Schuster Special
Sales at 1-866-506-1949 or business@simonandschuster.com.
The Simon & Schuster Speakers Bureau can bring authors to your live event. For more information
or to book an event, contact the Simon & Schuster Speakers Bureau at 1-866-248-3049 or visit our
website at www.simonspeakers.com.
Back matter artwork by Drew Willis © Simon & Schuster
Book design by Krista Vossen
The text for this book is set in Melior.
Manufactured in the United States of America • 0810 FFG
Library of Congress Cataloging-in-Publication Data
Barber, Tiki, 1975–
Red zone / Tiki Barber and Ronde Barber with Paul Mantell.
p. cm.
A Paula Wiseman Book.
Summary: Identical twins Ronde and Tiki Barber's excitement over the
approaching state championship football game turns to worry when there
is a chicken pox outbreak at Hidden Valley Junior High.
ISBN 978-1-4169-6860-3 (hardcover)
1. Barber, Tiki, 1975—Childhood and youth—Juvenile fiction.
2. Barber, Ronde, 1975—Childhood and youth—Juvenile fiction. [1. Barber,
Tiki, 1975—Childhood and youth—Fiction. 2. Barber, Ronde,
1975—Childhood and youth—Fiction. 3. Football—Fiction. 4. Chicken
pox—Fiction. 5. Schools—Fiction. 6. Twins—Fiction.
7. Brothers—Fiction.] I. Barber, Ronde, 1975– II. Mantell, Paul.
III. Title.
PZ7.B23328Red 2010   [Fic]—dc22
2009050976
ISBN 978-1-4424-0947-7 (eBook)

FIRST
EDITION

ACKNOWLEDGMENTS

The authors and publisher gratefully
acknowledge Mark Lepselter for his help in making this book.

EAGLES' ROSTER
8TH GRADE HIDDEN VALLEY JUNIOR HIGH SCHOOL

HEAD COACH—SAM WHEELER
DEFENSIVE COACH—PETE PELLUGI
OFFENSIVE COACH—STEVE ONTKOS

QB
CODY HANSEN, GRADE 9
MANNY ALVARO, GRADE 7

RB
JOHN BERRA, GRADE 9
TIKI BARBER, GRADE 8
LUKE FRAZIER, GRADE 7

OL
PACO RIVERA (C), GRADE 8

DL
SAM SCARFONE (DE),
GRADE 9
IAN ROBERTSON (DE),
GRADE 7

LB
RICKY RUSSELL, GRADE 9
GARY LITTMAN, GRADE 9

WR
FRED SOULE, GRADE 9
JOEY GALLAGHER, GRADE 9, HOLDER

CB
RONDE BARBER, GRADE 8
BILL REEVES, GRADE 9
JUSTIN LANDZBERG, GRADE 7

S
MARK ZOLLA, GRADE 9
ALISTER EDWARDS, GRADE 7

K
ADAM COSTA, GRADE 8

CONFERENCE SCHEDULE

WILLIAM BYRD JUNIOR HIGH BADGERS—GAME 1 (HOME) — L 20–21
PATRICK HENRY JUNIOR HIGH PATRIOTS—GAME 2 (AWAY) — L 7–14
MARTINSVILLE JUNIOR HIGH COLTS—GAME 3 (HOME) — W 48–3
NORTH SIDE JUNIOR HIGH ROCKETS—GAME 4 (AWAY) — W 31–28
PULASKI JUNIOR HIGH WILDCATS—GAME 5 (HOME) — W 38–3
MARTINSVILLE JUNIOR HIGH COLTS—GAME 6 (AWAY) — W 34–17
BLUE RIDGE JUNIOR HIGH BEARS—GAME 7 (HOME) — W 30–10

REMAINING GAMES

JEFFERSON JUNIOR HIGH PANTHERS
EAST SIDE JUNIOR HIGH MOUNTAINEERS
BLUE RIDGE JUNIOR HIGH BEARS
WILLIAM BYRD JUNIOR HIGH BADGERS
NORTH SIDE JUNIOR HIGH ROCKETS

CHAPTER ONE

THE HEAT OF BATTLE

"PLAY PROUD, TIKI!"

More than 1,000 football fans were screaming their lungs out—but somehow, Tiki Barber was able to hear his twin brother's voice.

"Play proud!!!!"

Everyone knew Tiki was about to get the ball. It was third and two, with his team in the red zone at the Rockets' eighteen yard line. Who else would the Eagles give the ball to but their star running back?

Tiki settled into his three-point stance. "I hear you, Ronde," he muttered, digging his spikes into the ground to get a good jump.

"Twenty-five...seventy-three...hut-hut!" Quarterback Cody Hansen took the snap from Paco Rivera. Tiki lunged forward, and Cody rammed the ball smack into his midsection. Clamping down on it with both arms, Tiki stutter-stepped left, looking for an opening in the North Side Rockets' defense.

There it was! Right between Paco and John Berra, the

fullback. He darted through the tiny gap, and was almost into the open backfield when—THWUMP!

The next thing he knew, Tiki was airborne. He landed hard, with five hundred pounds of North Side defenders piled on top of him.

He could barely breathe, let alone tell them to get off! It seemed like forever before the refs pulled the pile away and Tiki could exercise his lungs again.

Getting up, he saw that he'd been tackled a yard short of a first down. Tiki grabbed his face guard and groaned. Now the Eagles would have to kick the ball away *again*. Their third punt already, and it was still the first quarter!

Tiki jogged back to the bench and sat down next to John Berra, his partner in the backfield. They watched as Adam Costa nailed the punt high and long, pinning the Rockets inside their own ten yard line.

"Way to go, Adam!" Tiki screamed. "You're the man!"

"Nice kick!" Berra called weakly.

"Yo, what happened on that last play?" Tiki asked, rubbing his sore left side.

"Huh? Sorry, what'd you say, Tiki?"

"The *block*, man. You're supposed to pick up the middle linebacker *before* he gets to me."

"Oh. Yeah, right. Sorry," said Berra, sounding too tired to care.

John was usually a reliable blocker. But today was the first game of the play-offs—and suddenly, he was two steps slower. That was a big reason why the Eagles' ground game was going nowhere.

On first down, the Rockets threw a screen pass. Ronde got wiped out by a block, and the runner advanced the ball all the way to the thirty-seven yard line.

On the bench, Tiki groaned, then winced as he saw his twin get up slowly. "Shake it off, Ronde!" he yelled, and sure enough, Ronde did.

Tiki turned back to Berra. "What's wrong with you today? Were you up all night or something?"

Berra shook his head. "I dunno. I feel kind of weird for some reason."

"Since when?"

"I don't know . . . yesterday?"

"Well, go tell Coach about it."

"No way! Are you kidding me? I've waited all year to get here. I'm not sitting out now."

As if to make his point, John stood up and stretched. "I'm gonna get some water. Maybe that'll help." Raising a warning finger at Tiki, he added, "And don't you say anything either."

Tiki understood how John felt. Last year, and the year before that, the Eagles had made the play-offs only to fall short. For Berra, and for all the other ninth graders on the team, this was their last shot at a State Championship.

The Rockets were running now, ripping holes in the Eagle line and racking up the yards. Already they were in

Eagle territory, and Tiki was starting to get a bad feeling in his stomach.

The Eagles had barely squeaked into the play-offs this season. They'd beaten these same Rockets in their final game to get there—but that had been a real slushfest. A lot of balls had bounced the Eagles' way in that final game. But were they really better than the Rockets? It sure didn't look that way so far today.

This past week had been a nonstop carnival at Hidden Valley Junior High. Tiki smiled and shook his head as he remembered what it had been like—everyone at school bragging about their "Team of Destiny," saying how the Eagles were definitely going all the way this year. Tiki had let himself revel in the dream, and he knew his team-mates had done the same.

But now the time for dreaming was over. To become state champions, they would have to win their own district first. This was their opening play-off game, and *already* they were in trouble, down 6–0 with the Rockets looking for more. If the Eagles' play-off run ended today, it would be a gigantic, humongous comedown!

Tiki told himself to keep the faith. So many times this season, they'd faced elimination, yet somehow they'd survived. Could they do it one more time?

The Rockets threw a long pass, but Ronde batted it away. "Attaway, Ronde! Whoo-hoo!"

Turning, Tiki saw Berra wobbling slightly on his way

back from the water cooler. Something was definitely wrong with him—but *what*? He looked back just in time to see the Rockets run around end for a big gainer, all the way into the Eagles' red zone!

Uh-oh.

Adam Costa sat down next to him. "What's wrong, Tiki?" he asked. "You guys look totally lost out there on offense."

"I don't know," Tiki admitted. "Coach keeps yelling for us to pick up our blocks. But it's not happening."

"Yeah, what's with Berra? He's, like, in a daze."

Tiki looked down the bench to the far end, where Berra was sitting with his head between his knees. "Hmm. I'm gonna go talk to him."

Just then, the Rockets completed a short pass play over Ronde's outstretched arm for a touchdown.

"NOOOO!" Tiki cried, throwing back his head.

"Dang!" Adam said. "If only Ronde was a couple inches taller . . ." Then he caught his breath. "Oh. Sorry, Tiki."

Tiki and Ronde were identical twins, so their height was exactly the same. "It doesn't matter as much for a running back as for a corner," Adam added lamely.

Tiki sighed. What could he say? It was the truth. He and Ronde were two of the smallest guys on the team. If they didn't start growing soon, they might never get big enough to achieve their dream and play in the NFL.

But that was a problem for another day. Right now, he had a pep talk to give.

"Hey, John," he said, sitting down next to the fullback, "it's not just you. Cody's way off, I haven't found my rhythm—it's all of us, dude."

"Mostly me," Berra insisted. "I feel like a loser. I don't know what it is."

As he and Berra watched the extra point go through the uprights, the queasy feeling grabbed Tiki's stomach again. Sure, there was still plenty of time to turn things around and save their play-off run. But at 13–0, this game had all the signs of a terrible, final defeat.

The kickoff went up. Ronde grabbed it in the end zone and knelt down for a touchback.

Tiki gritted his teeth, jammed his helmet back on, and forced down the lump in his throat. *It can't end like this*, he told himself. *I won't let it.*

"Come on, dude," he said, grabbing Berra by the arm and lifting him to his feet. "Let's get back out there."

In the huddle, Tiki could see the hollow look in his teammates' eyes. He knew they were all scared—and why shouldn't they be? "Come on now!" he suddenly yelled, surprising himself as well as the rest of them. Tiki was not the type to yell at anybody. "Let's get some points here!"

"Okay, Texas Tech, on two," said Cody. That meant a screen pass for Tiki, with Berra as his lead blocker.

Tiki looked over at Johnnie B. Was he even listening? He looked dazed, and even more scared than the rest of them.

"Twenty-six . . . twenty-eight . . . hut! Hut!" Cody took the snap and dropped back. Paco and the rest of the line let the defense get past them, luring them in. Then, at the last moment, Cody threw the ball to Tiki, who was waiting by the sideline.

He took the pass and turned, just in time to see Berra go down to make a block. But the defender easily jumped over him and made straight for Tiki!

Tiki dodged him, but before he could get up a head of steam, he was brought down by two other Rockets.

"Berra!"

As Tiki dragged himself to his feet, he heard Coach Wheeler calling John, motioning for him to come to the bench. Berra trudged off, while Luke Frazier, the seventh grader who backed up both Berra and Tiki, ran onto the field, hopping up and down with excitement. It wasn't often he got a chance to play, especially in a big game.

I guess Coach finally noticed, Tiki thought. *About time, too.* Much as he liked Johnnie B., it was the game that mattered. Even Berra would agree with that.

Without their big fullback in the lineup to block— Luke was at least three inches shorter and thirty pounds lighter than Berra—Coach Wheeler directed Cody to go to the passing game.

7

It seemed to work at first. Cody connected on three passes in a row, the last one a long bomb to Fred Soule— another ninth grader playing for his legacy—for the Eagles' first touchdown.

One extra point later, the score was a respectable 13-7. Tiki began to get his hopes up. Six points wasn't that much to overcome—if only their defense could keep the Rockets from scoring again. . . .

The first quarter ended, and the second began. The Eagles' defense, led by Ronde and defensive end Sam Scarfone, now started to find its game. North Side managed three long field goal attempts, but only one went through the uprights, giving the Rockets a 16–7 lead.

The Eagles were still in the game, but their offense seemed dead in the water. Every time he tried to run, Tiki was met by a solid defensive wall. His blocking just wasn't there. Luke Frazier was a good athlete, but he was small and fast, like Tiki.

John Berra was big, strong, and usually a solid blocker. All season long, he'd been the one Tiki ran behind. Without Berra, against a huge defensive line like North Side's, Tiki was being stonewalled, and it was just getting worse as the half wore on.

When they tried to pass again, the Rockets were ready. They batted down three of Cody's tosses and intercepted two more, setting up two of those field goal tries. The Rockets were driving again when the half mercifully ended—not a moment too soon for the exhausted and discouraged Eagles.

Tiki ran for the locker room. It was the first time all day he'd run free of interference, and he wanted to be the first one in there. He banged open the door, and let out a scream of frustration that echoed in the empty room.

Except it *wasn't* empty. John Berra was already there, lying on one of the benches with a wet towel over his face.

Tiki went over and lifted the towel. Berra's eyes were closed, and his face was white as a sheet. "Whoa," Tiki said. "You look like crud, man."

"I feel like crud."

The door banged open, and the whole team filed in. One after the other, the Eagles dropped down onto benches, looking discouraged and beaten.

The last to enter was Coach Wheeler. He made one of his classic "entrances," slamming the door behind him on purpose so that everybody jumped. "Okay, that's enough of that! We just got our heads handed to us, am I right?"

A murmur of "yes" went around the room. Players stared at the floor or at their lockers. No one looked at one another, or at the coach. No one except Tiki, who knew Wheeler better than any of them.

Way back in seventh grade, he'd watched Mr. Wheeler in science class. Tiki had admired how he got kids' attention and motivated them to do better. And then, when Wheeler became their coach, Tiki had watched him establish his leadership over the team.

Tiki knew that this moment, right now, was one of those critical times when a coach can bring a team back from the edge of defeat. He believed in Wheeler, and he hoped the rest of the team did too.

"We were lousy out there. Every one of us—you might think you played better than somebody else, but believe me, you didn't. 'Cause we're a TEAM, get it? We lose together, and we win TOGETHER."

He let the room go silent, so they would all think about it. Then he said, "But we don't have to play that way in the *second* half. That was not the Eagle team I know. That was not the Eagle team that fought tooth and nail to get here today!"

A few of the kids said, "Yeah!" Others nodded, beginning to get their spirit back.

"Now, we get the ball first in the second half. If we can score—even a field goal—we can change the momentum of this game. But we cannot—we CANNOT—let ourselves be outplayed, or *outworked*."

He turned and said, "Berra, get that towel off your head."

John removed the towel. He looked *awful*. His skin was a pale gray-greenish, and his eyes were red.

Coach Wheeler went over to him and put a hand on

his forehead. "How long have you been sitting here?"

"Ten, fifteen minutes."

"You've got a fever, son," said Wheeler. "I'm going to find someone to take you home."

"NO!! Coach, no, I—"

"Don't mess with me, John. You've got a fever for sure. I want you to get home and get some rest."

"But the team! I can play, Coach. I'm fine, really!"

"Berra—"

"I'm NOT sitting out, Coach!" Berra said, standing up and grabbing Wheeler by the arm. "I'm playing! I *am*!"

Coach Wheeler looked at him sadly and shook his head. "To be honest, kid, you're not helping us any in your condition. I have to sit you down."

Tiki winced. Coach Wheeler was a straight-up guy, and Tiki really liked that about him. But he could some-times be *brutally* honest.

Johnnie B. choked up a little, but there was no arguing with Coach Wheeler.

"Now, are your parents here to take you home?" Wheeler asked.

Berra nodded, sniffing back tears and staring at the floor.

"All right, then. I'll have them sent for. You be ready to go in five minutes."

"Coach," Cody protested. "What are we gonna do without John?"

Wheeler frowned. "That's why we have *subs,* Hansen.

11

When things happen—and they always do—our subs have to step up and help the team."

He turned and looked straight at Luke Frazier. "You ready, kid?"

"Ready, Coach," Luke said, looking serious and intense.

"Good. Now all of you, listen to what I'm saying. These things happen—players go down—and that's when the rest of us have got to take it up another notch. We've got to step up for our fallen teammate!"

That got a cheer out of the Eagles—but Wheeler wasn't done.

"Now, I want you to get out there and give my man Luke here all the support he needs, so he can give *us* what *we* need. Remember what you're doing—stepping up for your teammates—that's the true test of a champion. . . . Do you want to be champions?"

"YES!!" everyone shouted.

"Then get out there and win this game for Johnnie B.!"

"YEAH!!"

"Get out there and make us all proud!"

"YEAH!!!"

"Get out there and take this game right out of their hands!"

"YEAH!!!!"

"Get out there and *make history*!"

A deafening roar shook the room as the Eagles

screamed and pounded on their lockers. Even Johnnie B., with tears in his eyes, gave it everything he had left.

They ran full-speed out onto the field, as the Hidden Valley faithful yelled their lungs out.

The kick went up, and Ronde was off and running the moment he caught the ball. He sped right at the onrushing Rockets. Then, just as he was about to smash into them head-on, he sidestepped, and found an open seam.

"Man, he's fast!" Fred Soule said to Tiki as they stood on the sideline. *"There he goes!"*

"All the way, Ronde!" Tiki shouted. "YES!!"

Ronde raised the ball to the sky as he crossed the goal line. Then he threw it into the crowd, and leaped into the arms of his teammates.

The second half was on!

The Eagles were bringing their "A" game now. After stopping the Rockets on three and out, they ground out a long drive and kicked a field goal to jump in front, 17–16.

But the Rockets weren't about to lay down and surrender. They quickly grabbed the lead back with a field goal of their own.

Tiki was still having trouble finding holes in the defense. Luke was trying his best, but he just didn't have Berra's size and experience. So Coach Wheeler kept relying on the passing game.

Another quarter passed, with neither team able to put

points on the board. The score was still 19–17, Rockets. The Eagles had given it their best, but now the clock was running out. With only two minutes left in the game— and maybe in their season—they got the ball back on their own thirty-four yard line. Time for one last desperate drive.

It did not begin well. On first down, Cody was sacked looking to pass to Fred, who never got free.

On second down, Cody threw a short pass to Tiki, who managed to get back only to the original line of scrimmage.

Now it was third and ten. "Mississippi State," Luke said, bringing the play in from the sideline. It was a pass play, going over the middle to Joey Gallagher. *Not a bad call*, Tiki thought—but the Rockets would surely be waiting for it.

"Cody," Tiki said as they huddled up, "how about sending me downfield?" His usual job on the play would be to stay in the backfield, in case of a blitz.

"What?"

"Downfield. Along with Fred. As in *way* downfield."

"We don't even have that in the playbook! You only catch short passes and run with the ball."

"Dude, trust me on this—they won't be looking for me to run a corner pattern." Tiki grabbed Cody by the arm. "You know how fast I am—I can get by those guys, you'll see! If you can't hit Joey, look for me out there."

"Do it, Cody," Joey said, nodding. "He's right. They're all over me, double-teaming me every time. And Tiki's the fastest guy on the team, except maybe for Ronde."

Cody's mouth curled into a grin. "Let's go for it!" he said. "On three."

The play clock was almost down to zero by the time they snapped the ball. Tiki faked a block, then ignited his burners. He saw the safety double-teaming Joey, just as they'd expected. Meanwhile, Fred had taken his man to the middle, while Tiki ran down the far sideline, wide open.

Cody faked the pass to Fred Soule, looked for Joey and saw he was double-covered—then turned and saw Tiki, wide open on the opposite side of the field. Cody hurled the ball as far as he could throw it.

The ball sailed toward Tiki, a perfect spiral, and he grabbed it in full stride. The safety saw what was happening, but he arrived three steps too late. Tiki was already in the end zone!

After the celebration and the extra point, the score was 24–19, Eagles. The offense ran triumphantly off the field, only to have Coach Wheeler scold them, saying, "Hey! HEY! Can the celebrations—this game's not over yet!"

But Tiki could tell he was pleased by the on-field adjustment they'd made. Coach Wheeler liked his players to be thinking out there, taking advantage of opportunities.

There were still thirty-five seconds left. The Rockets ran Adam's kickoff back to midfield, then went to work, using their three time-outs and some quick out patterns to drive into the Eagles' red zone, with time for one more play.

"Hold 'em, Ronde!" Tiki screamed, his voice hoarse after too much shouting.

This was the play that would decide the game, and with it, the Eagles' future—or lack of it.

The Rocket quarterback rolled to his right. The Eagle defenders chased him—but suddenly, he handed the ball to his wide receiver, who was going the opposite way!

"End around! End around!" Tiki shouted, but nobody heard him.

Luckily, Ronde saw the trick, just in the nick of time. He reversed direction and ran down the ball carrier from behind, knocking him out of bounds just short of the goal line!

The gun sounded. Everyone yelled their guts out.

Game over! The Eagles had lived to fight another day!

CHAPTER TWO

FOOTBALL FEVER

"GIMME FIVE, BARBER!"

Ronde raised his hand to be slapped. It was already sore, and he'd gotten to school only five minutes ago. Sure, everybody was all pumped up about the Eagles' come-from-behind victory. But did they have to smack him so *hard*? For them, it was one slap. For his poor hand . . . well . . .

The next time someone greeted him, he put out his left hand instead.

It had been a great morning, all in all. The Eagles had come so far, against the odds—and the excitement was obviously contagious. Football fever had gripped Hidden Valley Junior High and was now a totally out-of-control epidemic.

Ronde couldn't fully get into the celebration, though. For him, the fight wasn't over. After all, they hadn't actually *won* anything yet. Only when they held a trophy in their hands could they really be called champions.

He remembered the faces from yesterday's game—the pain in the eyes of the defeated Rockets as they watched the Eagles celebrate. Their slow walk off the field, staring at the ground as they went.

That could have been him, and Tiki, and all the rest of the Eagles, Ronde knew. The game could easily have gone the other way. Their season could *still* end in defeat—in fact, the odds of them winning the district championship were only fifty-fifty. And as for the state crown? Well, Ronde's best subject was math—and he knew those were some very long odds.

So he accepted the high-fives and backslaps with a smile. But he stayed cool about it, out of a healthy respect for lady luck, the football gods, or whatever made the ball bounce your way.

Still, as the morning wore on, Ronde found himself giving in to the general excitement. He kept replaying the highlights of their latest victory in his head. Twice in English, Ms. Kowalski called on him while he was in a daze, and the whole class laughed.

Normally, Ronde would have been horrified. But today, he didn't mind. The other kids knew where his mind was, because they were thinking about it too. Even Ms. Kowalski didn't seem annoyed, the way she usually was when kids didn't pay attention.

By lunch period, Ronde was in a really fine mood. Joining his teammates at their usual table, he felt like the big game had just ended. They all exchanged hugs and back-slaps, and began giving each other a hard time about the mistakes they'd made during the game—mistakes that were only funny now because they hadn't mattered in the end.

"Dude, that dance you did in the end zone needs some work," Paco told Tiki, demonstrating the way a *real* victory dance should look. Everyone howled at his antics. Paco was definitely the funniest guy on the squad.

"Hey, Tiki," said Joey Gallagher. "You looked like a rubber ball, bouncing off those big linemen."

"I know, man. That's what happens when your blocker takes the day off with a fever."

"You got that right," Cody agreed. "Did you see Berra's face in the locker room? He was *green*."

"He must have eaten something really bad," Sam Scarfone said, "'cause he's *still* out sick."

"Geez," Ronde said, his smile slowly fading. "I hope it's nothing really bad."

"Ah, he'll be okay," Paco said. "You know Johnnie B. He'll eat anything."

Everyone laughed, and that lightened the tension. But only for a minute—because that's when Adam Costa showed up, carrying his tray from the food line, and looking really worried.

"Hey, guys," he said, sitting himself down and heaving a sigh. "Did you hear the news about Berra?"

"What news?" Cody asked.

"You haven't heard? Nobody here knows about it?"

"About what?" Ronde demanded.

Adam gave the whole table a dark look. "We've got a great big problem, guys. Johnnie B.'s got chicken pox."

"Say *what*?" Tiki said.

"Yeah, I happened to pass by the nurse's office, and she was talking to Coach, so naturally I couldn't help overhearing. She told him it's going around the whole school, and that there's no telling who might come down with it next."

"Not me," said Cody. "I already had it once, back when I was little. You can't get it twice."

"Whew," Luke said. "That lets me off. I had it when I was a baby."

"Me too," said Joey Gallagher. "Thank goodness."

A few others chimed in, pretending to wipe the sweat off their brows in relief. But four or five kids just sat there looking worried.

Ronde glanced over at Tiki, who was staring right back at him. They were thinking the same exact thing, as they often did.

Neither of them had ever had chicken pox.

Worse still, Tiki ran in the backfield with John, and they hung out together at practice. Ronde had the locker next to Berra's. Were they doomed to be the next victims?

"Well, how long does it last?" Cody asked. "Will John be able to play in the district final?"

"Don't ask me," Adam replied. "I'm no doctor. I faint at the sight of blood."

"Man," Sam Scarfone said, shaking his head. "I hope

nobody else on the team goes down. I'd hate to lose out on a championship because of some stupid disease."

Nobody else said a word. The prospect was just too scary.

For the rest of that afternoon, Ronde went through his classes in a daze. Not the happy daze of that morning, but the doomed daze of a man walking to his execution.

Every chance he got, he looked at his reflection in the mirror or the window. He kept checking his arms for spots, but he didn't find any, even though he felt itchy all over.

He wondered if that was a sign you were about to get chicken pox.

He looked to the front of the classroom, where Mr. Murray was droning on about the particles of the atom. In the second row, Paco Rivera was squirming in his chair. Ronde saw him reach under his shirt and check for bumps.

In the fourth row, Bill Reeves, the team's other starting cornerback, had his hand on his forehead, checking for fever. He was trying to act normal, but Ronde knew the truth. Bill and Paco were as freaked out as he was.

And why was his heart thumping so loudly in his chest? Ronde was sure the whole class could hear it. He wondered why no one turned around to see where the hammering was coming from.

Ronde was sweating now, but he didn't have a fever—it was a cold sweat, from the sheer terror of getting sick.

This is ridiculous, he told himself. *I can't be worrying about this all week long.*

But much as he tried to talk sense to himself, his self wasn't listening.

Everyone knew chicken pox was highly contagious. There were fifty-five kids on the team, and all of them shared a locker room with Berra. What were the odds that none would get sick?

Close to zero, Ronde figured. Whether he himself caught chicken pox or not, he felt sure that Berra would not be the Eagles' last victim.

And the district championship final was less than a week away!

CHAPTER THREE

EXPOSED!

TIKI SLEEPWALKED THROUGH HIS AFTERNOON classes. He felt cold, but his armpits were wet with sweat. He wondered if that was a sign of chicken pox.

Everything seemed like a sign of chicken pox, at least to him. For instance, it couldn't have been an accident that today's history class was about the black plague.

"It was a *terr*ible time," Ms. Abdul-Malik was saying. "First, people would notice a swelling in their armpits. . . ."

Tiki checked his pits. Nothing . . . *yet.*

". . . Then they would get a fever, with *huge swellings* everywhere. . . ."

Tiki felt his forehead. He couldn't tell if it was warm or cool.

He cast a quick look around the classroom. Nobody else seemed the least bit worried about catching the plague—er, chicken pox.

Of course *they* weren't worried. If any of them came down with it, they'd miss a few days of school. Big deal—they'd stay home, relax in bed, eat ice cream, and watch TV. *Boo-hoo for them,* thought Tiki.

But for *him*, the stakes were much higher. Next Tuesday night, the Eagles would play for the *district championship*. It would be the biggest game of his entire life!

Sure, the Eagles had won the district last year, when Tiki and Ronde were still seventh graders riding the bench. But *this* year, the Eagles would be relying heavily on the Barber twins to power them past the mighty Pulaski Wildcats. If either he or Ronde—or for that matter, *any* of the Eagles—had to miss the game, the whole team might go down in flames!

After school, Tiki headed downstairs to get ready for practice. He sat down at his locker—right next to John Berra's empty one—and suited up.

Everyone on the team had the identical haunted look. They were all dreading the same thing. The ones who'd never come down with chicken pox had *all* spent the last twenty-four hours looking for telltale spots, and scratching imaginary itches. Those who'd already had it were worried about those who hadn't.

Either way, it was an awful feeling.

"Okay, let's get out there!" Coach Wheeler said, clapping his hands to snap them out of their daze. "Let's focus on the task at hand—we've got a game to win, guys!"

The team went through its paces, throwing themselves

into practice like a bunch of maniacs. It felt good, Tiki thought, to get his mind off his fears for a couple hours and concentrate on the game he loved.

"Stay down in your stance," he told Luke, who was standing in for Berra at fullback. "If you straighten up too much, they'll push you around. Here, let me show you. . . ."

Tiki demonstrated the proper technique to the rookie. Luke got the idea quickly—he was obviously a fast learner—but he still had a lot of growing to do before he could block like Berra. Another twenty pounds of muscle, and he'd be just fine. But that wouldn't happen overnight.

Hopefully, by next season Luke would be ready to take over at fullback. For now, though, he was just a fill-in. Tiki could tell he was nervous about having to play in the championship game.

"Hey, listen, I've been where you're at," Tiki told him, putting an arm around Luke's skinny shoulders. "Don't sweat it—you're gonna be fine, you'll see. Johnnie goes down, you step up. And we'll all be pulling for you, pick-ing you up if you make a mistake." There was an awk-ward silence before Tiki added, "Hey, who knows, maybe Johnnie B. will be back by game time."

"Let's hope so," said Luke glumly. "How long does chicken pox last, anyway?"

"Hey!" Coach Wheeler broke in, overhearing. "Keep

your focus on football, men. No distractions allowed!"

Tiki knew Coach was right, but it was hard to keep your mind off something that scared you half to death.

That evening, Tiki and Ronde were just finishing up their homework for the week—their mom always made them do it first, before letting them go have fun—when the phone rang.

Ronde was busy writing something, so Tiki went to answer it. "Hello?"

"Hey, Tiki. What's up?"

"Johnnie B! How're you doing?"

"Better, man. No more fever. Just mad itching."

"That's good! I mean . . . it *is* good, right?"

"Yeah, definitely!" John said, sounding distinctly upbeat.

Tiki turned to Ronde, who was giving him a frustrated look. "His fever's down."

"Excellent!" said Ronde, pumping his fist. "Is he gonna play Tuesday?"

"You gonna play Tuesday?" Tiki repeated.

"Do cats have elbows? You know I'm playing!"

"For sure?"

"Dude. There's nothing that could keep me off that field."

"So the spots are gone and everything?" Tiki asked.

"Well . . . not really," came the reply. "They're actually

even more noticeable. But the doctor said by Tuesday I won't be contagious, so if the school clears me to play, I'm there."

"Oh. That's cool."

But would the school let him play?

Tiki knew how cautious grown-ups were about things like this. If John played, and somebody else on the team got sick, or if John got a relapse, somebody in charge would be in trouble.

"So, I guess we'll see you Monday?" Tiki asked.

"I don't know. Tuesday for sure, though."

"Fantastic. Stay cool, man."

"You too," said Berra. "Hey, how's Luke doing?"

"All right," Tiki told him. "He's gonna be good next season, I think."

"But he's not there yet, huh?"

"Well . . . he's not you, dude."

"Thanks, Tiki," Berra said. "Thanks for that."

"Hey, you're the man, brother. Get well soon, you hear?"

"I hear that. See you."

"See you."

Tiki hung up and turned to Ronde.

"Well?"

"He says he'll see us at the game."

Ronde shook his head. "He'd *better* be there. And he'd better bring his 'A' game with him. We're gonna need it."

"Amen to that," said Tiki. "And here's hoping nobody else goes down before then."

Cody snapped the ball, dropped back and handed the ball to . . . John Berra!

Tiki couldn't believe it. He looked down at his empty hands—hands that were supposed to be cradling the football. He looked up just in time to see Berra get hit by the onrushing Pulaski lineman—and fumble the ball away!

Tiki ran after it, but the ball remained tantalizingly beyond his grasp. Then he looked up to see a huge Pulaski player leaping at him, while another reached for the ball and snatched it!

"NOOOO!!!"

Tiki sat up in bed, breathing hard in the darkness, beads of sweat dripping down his forehead. *Just a dream . . . thank goodness.*

From across the room, Ronde stirred. "What's up?" he asked, yawning.

"Nothing. Go back to sleep."

"What are you yelling about?"

"*Nothing,* I said. Stop being so annoying!"

"*Mmmm . . .*"

Soon, Ronde was snoring softly.

Tiki was still sitting up, waiting for his heart to slow down. *What a nightmare!* He was sweating, even though it was cold in the room. Shivering, he got out of bed, went to the bathroom, and closed the door gently behind him. Then he flicked on the light and checked himself out in the mirror.

Any spots? Not that he could see. And he didn't *feel* sick, except for the shivering. That *could* mean he was coming down with chills and fever—*or* it could mean he was just scared out of his gourd.

Yeah, that was probably it, he decided. "Go back to sleep," he told his mirror image. "And quit dreaming about bad stuff."

Saying so was one thing, doing so was another. No sooner had he fallen back to sleep than the nightmares started up again. And they didn't stop until the sun rose and the new day began.

"You boys all right?" Mrs. Barber gave Tiki and Ronde her most suspicious look. "You're so quiet this morning."

"We're fine," Tiki assured her.

"Yeah, we're fine," Ronde echoed needlessly.

"I see." She got up from the breakfast table, went to the counter and picked up her purse. "Well, I'm off to work, then. You be sure to do these dishes. Don't be leaving them in the sink like last time, you hear?"

"No, ma'am," Tiki said dully.

"No, ma'am," Ronde repeated.

Pausing, she put the purse down again. "All right, what is it? Are you feeling sick?"

"We already told you, we're fine!" Tiki insisted, with a hint of annoyance. She had hit the nail on the head, as usual. Honestly, sometimes he thought she knew every single thought that went through their heads.

"Why are you both so down? You won this week, didn't you?"

"Yes," said Ronde.

"Did you get a bad grade or something?"

"No," said Tiki.

She sighed. "I give up. Listen, you two, I left dinner in the fridge, because I've got to go to that meeting this evening."

"What meeting?" asked Tiki.

"I already told you. Did you forget already, or were you not listening in the first place?"

"Oh, yeah, right!" Now it came back to him—she had helped the community stop the construction of a polluting factory nearby. Now the neighborhood residents were trying to get the area made into a park, and Mrs. Barber was once again leading the effort.

Tiki gave her a big hug. "I love you," he said, then stepped back to let Ronde have his turn. After she left, he turned to his twin. "You know what I think? If Mom doesn't let anything get her down, why should we?"

"Hmm," Ronde said with a grin. "I believe you're right about that."

"Come on, wanna throw the football around?"

"Sure. You know I can throw it farther than you."

"Can not."

"Can too."

Laughing, they headed outside, their cares forgotten for the moment.

It was only that night, as they lay in their beds with the lights out, that the fears returned to Tiki's mind.

"You awake?" he asked.

"Yeah, you?"

"What do you think, I'm talking in my sleep?"

"I *wish* I could sleep," said Ronde.

"Me too. How long did Adam say it could take before we got chicken pox?"

"Up to a week."

"How long since the North Side game?"

"Not that long. We could still get it," Ronde said.

"Shut up!"

"Why? It's true."

"Don't remind me."

"Any spots on you?"

"No, you?"

"No."

Tiki wanted to add, "Not yet," but he didn't need to. He knew Ronde was thinking exactly the same thing.

CHAPTER FOUR

SAFETY

IT WAS AN ANXIOUS CROWD OF EAGLES THAT gathered in the lunchroom that Monday. All eyes were focused on the double entrance doors, to see if John Berra was back. He'd promised he would return for the game on Tuesday, but that still gave him one more day, Ronde figured.

They finally gave up waiting. "I guess he's not coming," said Sam Scarfone.

"I guess," Paco agreed. "Well, no sense waiting any longer. I'm gonna eat." He tucked into his . . . his . . . his whatever-it-was. Something gray, gooey, and nasty-smelling.

"Dude," said Ronde with a grin, "what is wrong with you? You'll eat *anything*."

"Mmgfphgh?" Paco mumbled with his mouth full, as if to say, *What's wrong with gray goo? It's delicious!*

"Hey," Tiki said suddenly, frowning, "there are too many empty seats at this table."

They all got quiet, looking around at the faces of their teammates. "Who's missing?" Cody asked. There were usually ten of them who ate at this table every day. Today there were only eight. John Berra was obviously still out. And that left . . . who?

"Where's Zolla?" Sam asked.

It hit them all at the same time. Mark Zolla, a ninth grader and their starting safety, was missing from his usual place at the table. Funny how none of them had noticed—they'd all been so busy searching for Johnnie B.

They all looked at one another now, fearing the worst. "Anybody see him today?"

Nobody had. And nobody wanted to think about what this might mean for the team.

Trouble was, they couldn't *help* thinking about it.

At practice, their worst fears were confirmed. "John Berra will definitely be back tomorrow," Coach Wheeler announced. "But unfortunately, Mark Zolla is now out indefinitely—with chicken pox."

A low murmur of dread rolled through the locker room.

"I knew it!" Ronde whispered to Tiki, who was sitting next to him on the bench.

"*Now* what do we do?" Tiki wondered aloud.

"As for Berra, I'm not sure what we'll get out of him," Coach Wheeler continued. "He'll start the game, and we'll see how it goes. Frazier, you're going to be in there a lot, spelling him—at *least*."

Luke nodded slowly. All week, he'd been working on

his game as if his life depended on it. He seemed determined to show them all what he could do with a little playing time.

"What about Zolla's spot?" Ronde asked.

"Alister Edwards, you ready to step up?" Wheeler asked, turning to a small, skinny seventh grader who looked about ten years old.

Alister nodded excitedly. "I got this, Coach!" he said, and made everyone around him slap him five.

"Al's good. He can do the job," Tiki said when Ronde gave him a doubtful look.

"He looks like you could knock him down if you blew on him hard," Ronde said, frowning. He liked Alister, but the kid was even smaller than him or Tiki—probably weighed less than anyone else on the team!

"He's almost as fast as us," Tiki reminded his twin. "He's covered me pretty well in practice."

"We'll see," Ronde said, as they filed out onto the field.

Alister started out well, doing a good job covering the long routes Fred Soule and Joey Gallagher ran. He had good leaping ability as well as speed, and he knocked down a few well-thrown balls.

"Hey!" Cody yelled in mock anger. "Somebody get that kid out of the way! I'm trying to throw a touchdown here!"

The players laughed, happy that Alister was doing

such a good job stepping up. *Maybe Zolla's going down isn't such a disaster after all*, Ronde thought.

During their first break, he and Tiki chugged down some water and sat on the bench with the rest of the team. Next to them, Alister accepted the congratulations of the other players.

"Way to step in there, little dude!" Paco said, clapping him on the back. "Zolla will be lucky to get back on the field when he comes back!"

Alister laughed, turning red. "Thanks, guys," he said. "Ugh. I've gotta sit down." He plopped down onto the bench next to Ronde.

"Tired?" Ronde asked.

"Are you kidding?" Alister said. "I've never gotten this much work!"

"Good job, Al," said Ronde. "Man, you look beat. You're all red, too."

"I am?" Alister asked, his grin fading. "Yeah, I do feel kind of played out."

"You're sweating bullets," Ronde said. "Here, you could use a towel."

He tossed one to Alister, who dried his face with it. "Thanks, man."

Ronde looked closer at Alister's face. It was still red, but not like a minute ago. Some of the red areas had faded, leaving only small . . . *red* . . . *dots.* . . .

"Oh, no!" Ronde gasped. "Tiki, check this out."

Tiki looked over at Alister, and saw what Ronde was getting at. "Oh, no, no, no . . ."

"What?" Alister asked, his eyes growing wide. "What are you guys staring at?"

"Dude," said Ronde, shaking his head sadly, "you've got spots."

"No way!" Alister's hands flew to his cheeks.

"Way," said Tiki, backing out of germ range along with the others.

"Hey, Coach!" Ronde called. "C'mere—you're not gonna believe this."

Wheeler came over and squatted down in front of Alister, staring at the obvious with a pained look on his face. "I'm sorry, son. You've got to go straight home. Right now."

"But the game—"

"We'll figure something out. But you've got to stay away from the rest of the team. We can't afford to lose anyone else—not with the big game tomorrow."

Alister looked like he was about to cry. Five minutes ago, the kid had been on top of the world. His big chance, his moment of glory. Now, it was all crashing down on him. Ronde couldn't bear to *look* at him, it was so sad.

Slowly, Alister gathered his stuff, said a sad good-bye to his teammates, and headed for the locker room, with a somber Coach Wheeler right behind him.

"Okay, you birds, let's get back to work!" shouted Mr. Ontkos, one of the two assistant coaches. "Keep your minds on the game, boys—Pulaski isn't going to lay down and let you win just 'cause they feel sorry for you!"

Ronde knew it was true. The Wildcats of Pulaski Junior High had the best record of any team in the district. Way back in October, the Eagles had beaten the previously undefeated Wildcats by a whopping 38–3 score. But that was three months ago. Pulaski had lost only once since then. Two losses in a whole season—the best record in the league.

No one on the Eagles thought this game was going to be as easy as the last time. If Berra wasn't at his best, would Tiki be able to break big runs like the first time around? *Probably not,* thought Ronde. And what were they going to do for a safety, with both the starter and his sub out sick?

Coach Wheeler returned from the locker room and huddled with his two assistants. Ronde noticed them looking in his direction. Then Coach Ontkos called his name, and motioned for him to join them.

Ronde trotted over there. "What's up?" he asked.

"Barber," Coach Wheeler said, "how would you feel about starting at safety tomorrow?"

"Me?" Ronde gasped. "But—but I've never played safety!"

"I know that," said the coach, "but you and your brother are the best natural athletes on the team. Besides, I've got two good subs at cornerback who can fill in for you—but I've got nobody to roam the backfield in place of Zolla."

Ronde was silent, looking down at the floor. All year, he'd played the corner position, guarding the best receiver the opposing team could throw at him, one-on-one, *mano a mano*.

But safety was a whole different animal. You stood back there, waiting and watching the play develop. You let the receivers start their patterns, and then you had to decide which one to cover. You had to watch the quarterback, too, to see where he was about to throw the ball. And finally, you had to get there before the ball did so you could break up the play.

"Ronde?" Coach Wheeler said gently. "The team needs you to do this. I know it's not what you want. But it's the only shot we have to plug the hole at safety and win the district championship. So . . . what do you say?"

Ronde looked up at the coach, his jaw set, and nodded. "I've got it covered, Coach," he said firmly.

"Atta boy," said Wheeler, clapping him on the back. "I knew you'd step up. And I know you're gonna have a great game tomorrow." He offered him his hand, and Ronde shook it. "Okay, then. Get back out there, and let's give you a few reps at your new position."

Ronde nodded, and put his helmet back on. As he turned to go, he heard Wheeler calling him.

"And Barber—"

"Yes, Coach?"

"Remember, what you're doing—stepping up for your fallen teammates—that's the true test of a champion."

Ronde sighed deeply, then jogged back out onto the field. Maybe Coach was right. Maybe he would do great at safety in tomorrow's game.

But what if he didn't? What if he made a mess of a position he'd never learned to play? What if he totally cost the Eagles the game!?

Even worse, what if he never even *made* it that far? Hadn't he just been hanging around with Alister, breathing in all those germs? Why, he might even break out in the dreaded spots by game time tomorrow!

Ronde sighed. Wouldn't that be just his luck?

Somehow, though, his luck held out, and so did Tiki's. They made it to the game without a single spot between them. Sitting next to each other on the bus to Pulaski, they counted heads. They were relieved to find that everyone but the two sick safeties was on board. "At least there's no new bad news to deal with," Tiki said.

"And we've got Berra back," Ronde pointed out.

"Yeah," Tiki said, then added under his breath, "but will he be the real Berra?"

"Time will tell," said Ronde. Then he thought, *And what about me, at safety?*

Well, time would tell about that, too.

• • •

Pulaski's fans were everywhere, jamming and overflowing the bleachers. The few Eagles fans who'd made the trip were seated in one far corner of the stands. Their voices were totally drowned out by the hordes of screaming Wildcat supporters.

Great, thought Ronde. *Just one more thing to make it even tougher. All right, bring it on, because we're not going home without that trophy.*

"We've come this far, boys," Coach Wheeler reminded them on the sideline. "If we win this game, we'll be taking home that nice big trophy, and it'll have all our names on it, now and forever, as district champions!"

After the cheering died down, he continued:

"I know we're underdogs today. Last time we saw these guys, we took 'em by surprise. This time, they're ready for us. It's gonna take everything we've got, but if we play our hearts out today, we *will win this game.*"

The Eagles let out a mighty roar and ran out onto the field, psyched to the hilt.

Ronde took the opening kickoff and ran it to the Wildcats' forty—great field position. But it quickly became obvious that John Berra was not back to full strength after all. He was a step slower than usual, at least, and a whole lot weaker. The Pulaski rush pushed him aside and stopped Tiki for short gains twice, then almost sacked Cody on third down.

Luckily, Coach Wheeler let them go for it on fourth down, and Cody got the first down on a quarterback draw. They didn't get much farther, but they did manage a field goal from the twenty yard line.

Not bad for starters.

After the kickoff, it was the defense's turn. Ronde lined up in the backfield, with the Wildcats starting on their own twenty.

This is so weird, he thought. Last time the Eagles and Wildcats had locked horns, he'd played man-for-man on Patrick Walsh, the Wildcats' best receiver, and stopped him cold all day. He knew he could do it again today, too.

But this time, his job was to watch not just Walsh, but all the other receivers as well—and they were no slouches either. Every time they broke from scrimmage and made their moves, Ronde would have to make a snap decision about where the ball was going to be thrown.

In their early-season matchup, the Wildcats kept trying to gain ground on the Eagles by running behind their huge lineman, Burt Golub. But the Eagles had double-teamed him, throwing a monkey wrench into the Pulaski attack.

This time, Coach Wheeler was guessing the Wildcats would try something different. He'd warned Ronde and Justin Landzberg, Ronde's sub at cornerback, to be ready for the long bomb on Pulaski's first drive.

Sure enough, that's what happened. Ronde was ready

for it—he'd dropped back about fifteen yards from scrimmage. Still, with his inexperience at safety, he had trouble guessing where the ball was going to be thrown. The quarterback faked him out to the weak side, then threw to Patrick Walsh for a twenty-five yard gain.

Two plays later, the same thing happened. Justin, left alone on Walsh, got burned for thirty-two yards on third and long.

"No!" Ronde screamed, but to no avail. The Wildcats were in the Eagles' red zone at the nineteen yard line, and driving. Ronde was sure they'd be looking to throw to Walsh again.

When the ball was snapped, and the quarterback rolled to the right, Ronde knew he could throw to only one corner of the end zone. Walsh's corner. Ronde held his ground, cutting off the run, daring the quarterback to throw it.

The moment the quarterback's arm went back, Ronde made his move. He got to the ball just in time to bat it away from the outstretched arms of Patrick Walsh.

Pulaski ran on second down, for no gain, thanks to a ferocious tackle by Sam Scarfone. Then, on third and ten, they passed again—and once again, Ronde was ready.

This time, he guessed, the quarterback would fake to Walsh and throw to the middle. He held back an extra instant, fooling the quarterback into thinking he could complete the pass. Then Ronde darted in front of the receiver, and made the interception in the end zone!

Mobbed by his teammates, Ronde broke free and ran for the sideline. He headed straight over to Coach Wheeler, who threw his arms around him.

"That's my man!" he yelled. "Way to go, Barber! I knew you could play safety!"

Ronde was happy, all right. But he also knew the game was just getting started. There were still more than three quarters to go. Sooner or later, he was bound to mess up at his new position. And what would happen then?

Deep in his heart, he was sure the only way to an Eagle victory was for Tiki to rack up enough points to cover the ones he, Ronde, was going to cost them.

"Come on, Tiki," Ronde muttered under his breath. "Break one big! Break one for *me*!"

CHAPTER FIVE

AN EPIC BATTLE

TIKI WAS GETTING TO KNOW THE WILDCAT defense very well. *Too well*, in fact.

John Berra and Luke Frazier were supposed to be keeping the huge Pulaski linemen off Tiki's back—but it wasn't working. They were getting pushed straight back into Tiki, or thrown out of the way like a couple of bowling pins.

So far, the Eagles' running game was going nowhere. Going to the air wasn't working either, since on passing downs, the Wildcats were coming at Cody with every blitz known to mankind—or at least, to junior high school football.

This was a far different Pulaski team than they'd faced early in the season. That team had been totally taken by surprise when the Eagles, prepped by Coach Wheeler with video of the Wildcats' weaknesses, came in better prepared and made short work of Pulaski, 38–3.

This time, it was the Wildcats who had come prepared. Everywhere Tiki went, he was shadowed by at least one linebacker. By the end of the first quarter, Tiki,

Cody, Coach Wheeler, and everyone else could see that the Eagles needed to change their game plan.

In other words, they were going to have to improvise if they hoped to come away with the district championship.

"Yeah, Ronde!" Tiki yelled from the sidelines as he watched his twin bat down another long pass.

"Man, he is having himself a day!" Cody said, slapping Tiki five.

"You guys!" Coach Wheeler called them over to his side. "Listen, we're going to have to change things up, and we can't wait till halftime."

"Right," Cody agreed.

"I'm down with that," said Tiki. "How about we run some plays for Luke? We could dump him some quick passes in the flat—no one's covering him, because they're double-teaming me."

"The rookie?" Cody said, looking downcast. "No way! He's not ready. Let's go to Berra."

"Berra's only at half-strength, in case you didn't notice," Coach Wheeler said to Cody. "I say we go to Luke. I think the kid deserves a chance—and you're right, Barber. They'll never see it coming."

He patted Tiki on the shoulder pad. "I wasn't sure it would be okay with you—I know you're used to being the man out there."

"That's okay, Coach," Tiki said. "Whatever gets us into the end zone."

"That's my guy," Coach Wheeler said. "Now let's go put some points on the board!"

They didn't have long to wait. On the very next play, Ronde picked off his second pass of the game. If he hadn't stepped out of bounds on the spectacular grab, he would have had an easy touchdown of his own.

"Dang!" he said as he passed Tiki and Cody on his way to the bench. "I should've scored on that play!"

Tiki high-fived his twin, laughing. Nothing was ever good enough for Ronde unless it was perfect. "You look out, now, Ronde," he shouted after him. "You keep this up, and they're gonna make you play safety every week!"

On first down at their own forty, Cody faked a handoff to Tiki. That was the last Tiki saw of the play, because he was immediately flattened by two Wildcats. The only thing was, he didn't have the ball—Luke did!

Tiki heard the cheering from the Eagles' fans in the far corner of the stands. "Get off me, you big lugs!" he said, trying to shove the defenders off him. Finally, he got to his feet, and saw his teammates rejoicing and chest-bumping each other.

"Touchdown!" Cody was yelling, his arms thrust high in the air like goalposts. "That's what I'm talkin' about!"

He clapped Tiki on the shoulder and said, "Good call, yo! Fantastic!"

Tiki headed for the sidelines, sore but happy. So what if it wasn't *him* scoring the touchdown? The Eagles were leading now, 10–0, and the pressure was all on Pulaski as the first half came to an end.

Coach Wheeler was excited, Tiki could tell. The way he kept bouncing around the locker room, encouraging his players, keeping it light and fun, trying to defuse the sense they all had that they'd been lucky so far.

Ronde had played out of his mind, with two unbelievable picks and who-knew-how-many batted-down passes. Luke Frazier had been an unexpected find, and they'd somehow managed to get around Berra's poor play.

But Tiki knew—and Coach surely knew—that Pulaski was not done yet, not by a long shot. It was all well and good for Coach Wheeler to be excited, and for the team to stay revved up and positive. But Tiki couldn't help feeling they were skating on thin ice.

Sure enough, the second half started out badly. Pulaski took the opening kickoff to their own thirty-five, then drove the ball on the ground, with their two star running backs, Marty Maris and Chris Tullo, leading the way. Those two took turns chewing up yardage until the Wildcats scored a touchdown—without throwing a single pass!

After stopping the Eagles cold and forcing them to punt, Pulaski used the same tactics on their next drive, running behind Burt Golub and wearing down the Eagle defensive line—especially Sam Scarfone, who had been getting double-teamed all day and was starting to look tired. Although the Eagle defense bent, they didn't break. Pulaski settled for tying the game with a short field goal.

On the Eagles' next drive, Cody made a mistake under the pressure of a blitz. Although he should have thrown the ball away, he tried to thread the needle to Joey Gallagher. The result was an interception that left Pulaski in charge in the Eagles' red zone.

Again, the defense made the Wildcats settle for a field goal. But now the Eagles trailed, 13–10. Tiki looked up at the scoreboard and couldn't help worrying. It wasn't a big deficit to overcome, three points. But the way things were going, and the way the momentum had shifted, those three points looked a whole lot bigger.

The Eagle offense continued to sputter, playing three downs and out all through the third quarter. Berra seemed like he wasn't quite over being sick. Tiki was suffering from the lack of blocking and the double-teaming, and Cody just couldn't get free to throw. As for Luke, the Wildcats were ready for him by now. Three times the Eagles tried to get him the ball, and each time, the defense was right there waiting.

Tiki thought he knew why. Luke was telegraphing things, tipping off the defense. He had a certain extra energy that told them he was the focus of the play.

Tiki could have shown Luke how to avoid that—but he couldn't do it in the middle of a game!

In spite of Adam Costa's long punts that pinned Pulaski deep in their own territory, the Wildcats kept running right at the Eagle defense—particularly Sam Scarfone. Normally, Sam was like a brick wall, and teams tried to run anywhere but in his direction. But now, the Wildcats were making him look very human. Early in the fourth quarter, they marched eighty yards on the ground, and were knocking on the door again with third and goal to go from the eight yard line.

The Eagles were expecting a pass, naturally, but to everyone's surprise, the quarterback faked the handoff, spun to the weak side, and threw a no-look floater to the corner of the end zone.

"Ronde!" Tiki shouted in alarm.

But he needn't have worried. If everyone else was surprised, Ronde wasn't. He played it perfectly, keeping stride for stride with the fullback, Chris Tullo, coming out of the backfield.

Tullo was six inches taller at least—but Ronde could out-jump just about anyone. He leaped, arms out-stretched, with perfect timing, and came down with the interception in the end zone—his third of the day!

Tiki and the rest of the Eagles leaped into the air, whooping with joy. "Now it's *our* turn," he told Cody. "I'm gonna break one this drive. You watch."

"How're you gonna do that, Barber?" Cody said. "You've got no blocking."

"Just *give* it to me on a passing down, when they won't be ready for it. I'll do the rest."

Cody hesitated. "You sure?"

"Trust me on this, dude. It's now or never. Hey, Coach!" he motioned Wheeler over and asked him if they could try his idea of running on third and long.

Wheeler stroked his chin and nodded slowly, his mouth curling upward in a cagey grin. "Sounds like a plan, boys," he said. "Go get 'em."

Cody started out with a couple of quick passes that got the Eagles near midfield. Then he tried a handoff to Tiki, which the Wildcats stifled for a two-yard loss. After a quick dump-off pass on second down to Luke, the Eagles faced a third and seven from their own forty-six.

With less than seven minutes to play, Tiki knew the game was on the line. If they didn't keep this drive alive, the Wildcats would take over and grind the clock down to nothing, even if they didn't score.

It was *Tiki Time*.

Cody called the draw in the huddle, much to everyone's surprise.

"You're calling a run on third and long?" Fred Soule said. "They've been burying Tiki all day. Throw me an out pattern, Cody—I've got this."

"Draw play," Cody insisted, looking over at Tiki. "They won't be expecting it. Watch."

The team lined up, Cody snapped the ball, and dropped back as if to pass. Tiki moved like he was going to block. Then, as the rush got closer, he took the ball quickly from Cody and dashed right through the onrushing linemen. Stutter-stepping left, then right, he made a sudden dash forward and into the open backfield!

The Wildcat secondary was caught totally by surprise. All the Eagle receivers had gone long, taking their coverage with them. Tiki now had to avoid them in the open field. But with his speed and moves, that was much easier than barreling through a bunch of beefy linemen!

The roar of the crowd was matched in his ears by the rush of his own breathing and the hammering of his own heartbeat. His legs were a blur as he changed direction once, twice, three times, then finally outran one final defender, and leaped headlong into the end zone for the go-ahead touchdown!

Tiki's teammates practically carried him off the field, which was a good thing, because he was totally out of breath and exhausted.

"I told you, man!" Cody exulted, throwing an arm

around Tiki's shoulder. "I told you it would work!"

Tiki shook his head. He would have laughed if he'd had any breath left.

That was Cody for you—if someone else had a great idea, he'd always take the credit. But Tiki didn't care. He was just happy they'd scored.

Now, Pulaski had just one last chance to avoid going down to defeat. Because their passing game had gone nowhere all day, they stayed on the ground. That plan worked in a way, gaining good yardage on every play. But it cost the Wildcats precious time with the clock winding down. By the time they reached the Eagles' twenty-five yard line, there was only one minute left in the game.

"Go Ronde!" Tiki yelled at the top of his lungs. "You got this!"

Ronde didn't appear to hear him. He stood in the backfield, casting his gaze this way and that, trying to scope out the whole field in front of him.

Here came the play—another run!

They're afraid of him! Tiki realized. Ronde had gotten inside the Wildcats' heads. Even though the clock continued to run, they refused to throw the ball—at least not anywhere near where Ronde could get his hands on it. Instead, they ran right at Sam Scarfone, twice in a row—and ended up at the Eagle's five yard line.

Down by 17–13, with ten seconds left and deep in the

Eagles' red zone, Pulaski called their last time-out.

It was third and goal, and Tiki knew they'd *have* to throw the ball, or risk the game ending before they could run another play. Which meant the Eagles' future would be in Ronde's hands.

No better place, thought Tiki.

The quarterback snapped the ball, faked a handoff, then dropped back to pass.

But where was Ronde? Not in the end zone, as he had been before. No—this time, he came blazing in on a safety blitz, blasting through a big hole in the Wildcat line and leaping on the quarterback, sacking him back at the twenty yard line as the clock ran out!

"YES!!!" Tiki yelled.

Ronde had done it. The Eagles had won!

They were district champions!

All the way back to Hidden Valley, the Eagles laughed, sang, and relived the highlights of their glorious championship game. They passed the trophy to one another until everyone on the team had his chance to hold it, kiss it, shine it up, or whatever they wanted to do.

Tiki let himself enjoy the moment just like the rest of them. But inside, his happiness was lessened by the knowledge that he hadn't had a very good game—for him, at least.

Sure, that magical forty-yard run for the winning

touchdown would stay with him for the rest of his life. But what had he done the whole rest of the game? Nothing. Without Berra playing at his peak, and against the fearsome Wildcat defense, he'd only managed 30 yards, not counting that one great run.

In fact, if the Eagles had played it conventionally on their last drive, Cody would have thrown the ball into the teeth of the waiting Pulaski secondary, instead of putting it in Tiki's hands for the surprise draw play that won the game.

Tiki sure hoped by the time they started regional play-offs next weekend, Berra would be back to his old self. *He'd better be,* Tiki thought. And *should* be too—after all, how long could the effects of chicken pox last?

Not *that* long, Tiki hoped. Otherwise their two missing safeties would still be out of commission, and they'd surely have a tough time against that regional power-house, the Abingdon Junior High Owls.

Tiki glanced across the aisle of the bus to where Sam Scarfone was holding the trophy, examining the words on the golden plaque at its bottom. As Tiki watched, Sam handed the trophy to Cody, then slumped back into his seat and closed his eyes.

What's up with him? Tiki wondered. Sam hadn't played a very good game either. The Wildcats had run right at him—something no team had done with success all season long. There had been no trace today of that ferocious glare of Sam's that had scared every lineman in the league for the past three years.

Uh-oh, thought Tiki.

Was Sam going to be the next casualty of the epidemic that was sweeping the Eagles?

The next day, his worst fears were confirmed. Not only did Coach Wheeler announce that Sam had come down with the chicken pox, but, he also told the dejected Eagles, their two safeties would not likely be back for the game against Abingdon on Saturday.

The only good news at practice was the improvement in John Berra's game. The change was instantly noticeable. His blocks were stronger, his moves were crisper, his reaction time was shorter—in fact, he was his old self again. *Finally.*

Still, Tiki wondered if Berra's return would be enough. Their offense could score thirty points against Abingdon, but without Sam Scarfone anchoring their defensive line, and with Ronde playing out of position for the second week in a row, would the Eagles' defense be able to stop the mighty Owls' attack?

Abingdon had gone 11–1 in the regular season, and had obliterated their district competition in the play-offs. In winning those two games, they'd scored a combined ninety-two points—an incredible feat. At the same time, their defense had allowed only twenty points in those two games.

The Owls were likely to be their toughest opponent yet. And the Eagles would have to play them with one hand tied behind their backs!

CHAPTER SIX

A HOLE IN THE LINE

TIKI AND RONDE TRUDGED HOME FROM THE BUS stop together. The weather had turned cold, and they could see their breath making clouds in front of them as they walked.

Neither twin said much. What was there to say? Nothing good, that was for sure. Neither of them wanted to bum the other one out, but anything they said would be a downer for sure.

Mrs. Barber noticed right away. "What's the matter with you two?" she asked. "Are you feeling sick? Come on over here and let me feel your foreheads."

"Ma, we're not sick," Tiki told her.

"We're fine," Ronde said.

"If you're fine, then I'm Santa Claus," said their mother. "Now, which one of you is going to tell me what's going on?"

She looked Tiki straight in the eye—probably because he talked about twice as much as Ronde did.

"Aw, Ma," Tiki said. "We're gonna lose the game on

Saturday. Sam Scarfone's got the chicken pox, and so do two other guys."

"If not more by Saturday," Ronde added. "Who knows? The whole team could have spots by then. We might even have to forfeit!"

He and Tiki both sighed together. But their mom wasn't having any of that.

"You boys cut out this nonsense right now," she ordered. "The way you talk, you've already lost the game!"

"We *have*, Ma!" Tiki said. "How can we possibly win? It isn't fair!"

"You know, life isn't always fair—that's just the truth," she said, putting one arm around each of their shoulders. "But you can't let it get you down. You're a good team, and if you play proud, and give it everything you've got, then win or lose, you'll be able to hold your heads up when the game is done."

"Yes, Ma," the twins said together. But neither Tiki nor Ronde looked up from the ground.

"And don't give me lip service," she added. "You think about what I said. Nothing ever got done by folks moaning and groaning. You've got to go in with a winning attitude if you want to come out winners. You're still a great team, if you play like you know how."

"But Ma, the whole school is counting on us!" Tiki explained. "Everywhere we go, they're whooping and hollering, bragging about how we're gonna mop the floor with the Owls. . . ."

"If we lose, we'll be letting them all down!" said Ronde.

"Boys," said their mom, "in every football game, one team loses. And whatever team that is, the players have to live with it—and so do their fans. But if the players give it everything they have—if they play proud—then they can stay proud of themselves, win or lose."

"But—"

"Don't argue with me, Ronde. You boys just think about what I said. I've been around a long time—much longer than you—and I know it's true. If you want to have any hope of winning on Saturday, you'll make yourselves believe it too."

Every day that week was like the countdown to an execution. Everyone came to the lunchroom dreading to see if there would be some new empty seat where an Eagle had sat the day before. It was bad enough that Sam's seat was empty. He was one of the four or five best players on the whole team, and maybe the best on defense except for Ronde.

And Mark and Alister's seats remained empty too, which meant Ronde would be back at safety again. That wasn't so bad in itself—he'd played out of his mind in the Pulaski game—but it also meant that Justin Landzberg, a seventh grader with almost no game experience, would be filling in for him again at corner. . . .

Maybe they'd gotten lucky during the district championships. No, definitely, they'd been lucky. Not to mention that they'd been *incredibly* lucky to even get in the play-offs!

But this was different. They were in the regionals now, playing the best teams in all of western Virginia—teams they'd never seen before, except on some very impressive video. Teams that were scary good—like the Abingdon Owls. Winning this game without Sam and the others wouldn't just be lucky—it would be a near-miracle.

On Thursday, and again on Friday, Tiki and Ronde called Sam at home, just in the hope that, somehow, he was getting well ahead of schedule.

"Yesterday I had a fever of 102," he told them. "Today it's down to 101."

"Good!" said Tiki.

"That's great!" Ronde added hopefully. "Right?"

"Guys," Sam said, his voice catching. "Let's get real— I'm not gonna make it tomorrow. Just . . . just win one for me, will you?"

"Sure thing, man," Ronde promised.

"You got it, Sam," Tiki said.

"Because if we lose . . ." Sam's voice trailed off into a terrible silence.

Neither Tiki nor Ronde said a word. They both knew

what Sam would have said if he wasn't busy choking back tears. He would have said, "If we lose, it'll be the end of everything—and it'll be *all my fault.*"

"You hang in there, Sam," Ronde finally said. He remembered what his mom had told them. "We're gonna play proud tomorrow—and we're gonna take it home for you."

"Truth," Tiki added.

And that was all there was to say.

Before the big game, Coach Wheeler gathered the Eagles together to psych them up. Tiki and Ronde were ready, having spent all week digesting their mother's advice. Ronde had realized somewhere along the line that she was right—and he knew Tiki had too. They'd both come to play football today, and each was prepared to leave everything they had on the field.

Still, most of the other Eagles looked down in the dumps. In addition to their sense of dread, they kept checking out one another's faces, hoping not to find any spots.

"Listen up, Eagles," said Coach Wheeler. "Great teams are great because their players always pick each other up. When one guy goes down, another steps up and holds the fort till he can get back."

He motioned to Tiki and Ronde. "Look at the Barbers if you want to know what I mean. Look at how Tiki stepped up last week, with that big run at the end of the game. Even though they double-teamed him, he managed to find a way to score. And Ronde—well, what can you say about a kid who's never played safety before, and then steps up the way he did? How many big plays did he make?"

An approving murmur went around the locker room. "A lot, that's right," Wheeler continued. "And Cody kept his wits about him all game. I know you all played your hearts out, and that's why we're here today.

"So, we haven't got Sammy. We haven't got Mark or Alister. But we've still got all the rest of us, and that's got to be enough." He looked at each one of them in turn. "Now, tell me—have we got it in us to win this game?"

"Yeah!" came the response, loud but not deafening.

"What? I can't hear you!"

"Yeah!" Louder this time.

"What's that you say?"

"YEAH!" The whole room shook with noise, added to by half of them banging on their lockers.

"Then let's go out there and take this game!" Coach Wheeler shouted over the din.

The Eagles poured out of the locker room and onto the field, running at full speed and shouting their war cry.

The game was on!

Ronde took the opening kickoff and ran it all the way out to midfield. From there, the Eagles offense went to work.

Behind a ferocious block from John Berra, Tiki broke a big run right off the bat. Before the game was five minutes old, Cody had thrown a dart to Joey Gallagher for a touchdown!

Ronde let out a big whoop from the sideline, and slapped five with the rest of his teammates on the defense. "Let's go!" he yelled as he led them charging out onto the field. They were fired up now. For the moment, all their worries had flown right out of their heads.

But the Abingdon Owls were famous for their fearsome offense, and now they showed why. They ran right through the Eagles' line for big gains, hitting hard at Sam's replacement, seventh grader Ian Robertson. They kept on running, not passing much at all, until they'd rammed the ball into the end zone for a tying score.

From that time on, the game became a slugfest, with the teams trading touchdowns on almost every drive. Both the Eagles and Abingdon were running the ball at will. With Cody mixing in the occasional pass, the Eagles had twenty-eight points by halftime.

The only problem was, so did the Owls.

By the time the fourth quarter rolled around, the score was a hefty but still tight 49–42 in favor of the Eagles, with the Owls driving for the tying score yet again.

Ronde and his fellow defenders were exhausted. So he was glad when Coach Wheeler called two time-outs in a row. Some might have called it foolish, because those time-outs were likely to be needed at the end of the game. But Ronde saw the wisdom in Wheeler's move. He was giving his defenders a chance to catch their breath—hoping that it would give them the strength to finally—for the first time—stop the Owl assault.

During the time-outs, Tiki ran over to Ronde's side with a wet towel to cool him off. It was a warm day for December, and the heat was tiring everybody out.

Ronde was breathing hard and sweating like a water fountain. "Thanks, Tiki," he said.

"You all right?"

Ronde just kept blowing out breaths of air, trying to get his wind back.

"Just stop them *this once*, Ronde," Tiki said. "If we get the ball back, I'll make sure we put this baby out of reach."

"I'll try," Ronde said, still panting.

"Whatever it takes, yo." Tiki clapped his twin on the back. "This is your moment. It's *Ronde time*."

Ronde nodded, and Tiki trotted back to the bench as the ref blew the whistle for play to resume.

The Owls were in the Eagle red zone, with third down and four to go at the fourteen yard line. Coach Ontkos had positioned his cornerbacks close to the line of scrimmage, to prevent any short passes. Only Ronde stood back in the end zone, in case the Owls chose to go for broke on the play.

And that's just what they did. After faking a handoff, then faking a quick pass to a closely covered receiver at the eight, the Owls quarterback ran to his right, and lobbed a floater into the far corner of the end zone.

Luckily, Ronde had been shadowing the quarterback's every move, and was fast enough to get to the ball in time.

The receiver was much taller, but Ronde made up for it by his amazing leaping ability. They both grabbed the ball—but when they fell to the ground, it was Ronde who still had his hands on it!

The Eagle crowd went berserk, yelling and hugging each other, and jumping up and down so much that the bleachers started shaking.

Ronde was so winded that he took a knee on the kick-off. Then he trudged off the field and collapsed onto the bench. His job was over, at least for now. He could sit there, catch his breath, and watch Tiki and the offense try to put the game away.

After the runback, it was Eagles ball at their own twenty, with five minutes left to play. Coach Wheeler ordered Cody to stay on the ground—which meant that it was up to Tiki to make first downs while the clock ran down to zero.

This was Tiki's moment—but it was also John Berra's finest hour. In his three-year career at Hidden Valley, he had never played with this much intensity and passion. Play after play, he pushed the defenders around, making

65

room for Tiki to sneak through holes and gain precious yards. Slowly, the Eagles moved the ball down the field, while Pulaski had to use up their precious time-outs one after the other.

Finally, with just thirty seconds left, and the Eagles facing fourth and seven at the Owl twenty, Coach Wheeler called in the kicking unit. "Old Reliable" Adam Costa split the uprights for the field goal that put the game out of reach, 52–42.

As the gun sounded, Ronde whooped with joy, threw his towel in the air, and ran to hug his brother. They led their happy teammates off the field as the Eagle fans poured out of the stands to greet their heroes. Incredibly, the Eagles had survived to fight another day!

"You see, boys?" Coach Wheeler told the happy, exhausted team when they finally made it back to the locker room. "You see what happens when everybody steps up and does his part? This was a team victory today, so the game ball goes to each and every one of you."

The team gave themselves a huge cheer, with hugs and backslaps all around.

"I'll tell you something else, Eagles," said Wheeler. "Whatever happens from here on out, to me, you'll always be winners. This season isn't over—not by a long shot. But if you keep playing like you played today, I like our odds."

"Just call us the Giant-Killers!" said Tiki, high-fiving his twin so hard that Ronde's hand was numb for the next ten minutes. But he didn't care—it was a small price to pay for a huge victory!

CHAPTER SEVEN

UNDER PRESSURE

"HEY, TIKI! HOW'S IT COMING? WE GONNA GIVE 'em a beating next week?"

"Hey, Cootie," Tiki said, turning from his hallway locker to greet Cootie Harris, the Eagles' mascot.

Cootie followed the team to all their games, wearing a really silly-looking eagle suit, and flapping his wings whenever Hidden Valley made a big play. He was one of the team's biggest fans, naturally. And even though the players liked to poke fun at him, they also looked at him as a good-luck charm.

He and Tiki exchanged the team handshake, which consisted of a high five, a low five, and a hip-wagging wiggle, all topped off by a ferocious double high five.

Tiki's hands were already sore from slapping so many hands all week, and the week before that, too. Everyone at Hidden Valley had gone "Eagle crazy," dressing in blue and orange, the team's signature colors, and screaming the team chants between periods and in the lunchroom.

It was all a lot of fun, but things were starting to spin out of control. Now that the Eagles were district champs, all of Roanoke had begun to take notice. A man from the *Roanoke Reporter* had interviewed many of the team members, saying the article he was going to write would be on the front page, not in the school sports section!

Every morning, the kids on the school loudspeaker system would finish their daily announcements with "Go Eagles!" Even the principal, Dr. Anand, had caught the spirit, calling a special booster assembly after the Abingdon game, just to honor everyone's new heroes.

Tiki was glad about it, for sure. But underneath all the excitement, and partly because of it, he was becoming more and more uneasy. Everyone was pulling for the Eagles to go all the way to the state championship. And while rooting for a title was okay, a lot of people were starting to *expect* it.

That was a heavy burden for Tiki and the rest of the Eagles to bear. And as if that weren't enough, they had to worry about the chicken pox too!

"We're counting on you this weekend," Cootie told him. "How many touchdowns you think you'll get?"

"I don't know, Cootie," Tiki said uncomfortably.

"I'll bet you score at least three—maybe even four or five! I hear Charlottesville West has no defense."

"Oh, yeah?" Tiki doubted it. No team could have gotten this far without being really strong both on offense and defense. Cootie was just letting himself get carried away. Tiki didn't blame him, but he knew it was important for him and his teammates to focus on the game, not the hoopla and hype that went along with it.

"I've gotta go," Tiki said, shutting his locker and hoisting his bookbag onto his shoulders. "See you around."

"Go Eagles!" Cootie shouted after him, raising a fist.

"Go Eagles!" half a dozen other kids echoed, just to join in.

"Hey, Tiki," another boy yelled. "Sign my cast?" He held up his broken arm, and with his good hand offered a pen. Tiki took it and signed.

"Thanks," the boy said. "Wait till the kids in Spanish see this!" He took his pen back and bopped off down the hall, floating on air.

Tiki sucked in a worried breath. He was everybody's hero now. But if the Eagles lost this weekend, would he get blamed for it? One thing was for sure—he'd be letting down every kid in the whole school, and all the teachers besides.

"Shake it off!" he ordered himself, shaking out his whole body to get rid of the horrible thought.

But it was hard to forget the situation when everywhere you went, people were saying how psyched they were about what you were supposedly going to do in the next game.

Things reached fever pitch the day the article came out in the *Reporter*.

"Listen to this," Ronde said as they sat at the breakfast

table before school. "'The Hidden Valley Eagles are the new talk of the town. Under Coach Sam Wheeler, the team has conquered every obstacle thrown in front of it, steamrolling to the district title. The Eagles are now the sentimental favorites to bring home the state championship trophy.'"

"Favorites?" Tiki repeated, surprised. "How did he get that idea?"

"Don't know. Coach said Charlottesville West hasn't lost a game all season."

"I'd rather be an underdog, to tell you the truth. I'm getting a little spooked about it. You?"

"Totally," Ronde agreed. "It's like, if we win, it's no big deal, because that's what everybody expects. And if we lose . . ."

There was a long silence. Then Tiki asked, "You think we will?"

"Will what?"

"Lose."

"No, man. We're gonna win—we have to!"

"See, now that's what I'm talking about. We *have* to win, *or else*."

"True."

Another long silence. "Anyway, he says we're *sentimental* favorites," Ronde pointed out. "That's different than just plain favorites."

"How's that?"

"It just means everybody *wants* us to win."

"Not in Charlottesville, they don't."

"Well . . ."

"Keep reading."

"Okay. Here goes: 'The team's season started out as a full-fledged disaster. Before their first game was played, they lost their longtime coach, the great 'Spanky' Spangler, who moved on to coach Hidden Valley High School to a second-place finish in his first season.'

"'Spangler's replacement was Sam Wheeler, but by the time Wheeler found his footing with his new team, they were 0–2 and sinking fast. Somehow, he managed to turn them around, and the Eagles put together a long winning streak.'

"'Their season threatened to come apart for good when all-star kicker Adam Costa was lost to the team for weeks. If not for some fortunate losses by their rivals late in the season, it would have been all over for the Eagles. Somehow, they reached the play-offs—and have not looked back since.'"

"I like that," Tiki said, smiling. "That's good stuff."

"Yeah, well listen to this," Ronde said. "'Considering all the obstacles they've already overcome—including the epidemic of chicken pox now affecting the team—it is this reporter's considered opinion that the Eagles are a team of destiny. With all-stars Tiki and Ronde Barber at the top of their game, the betting here is that Hidden

72

Valley will soon be hoisting the state champions' trophy over their heads. To which let us all say amen, and GO EAGLES!'"

Ronde lowered the paper and stared at his twin. "Man, we'd better win on Saturday."

"You got that right," Tiki agreed, wiping the sweat off his brow—sweat that hadn't been there before Ronde started reading. "I'm starting to get a baaad feeling about this."

"I know just what you mean," said Ronde, nodding. Patting the paper, he added, "And this kind of stuff isn't making things any easier."

At Thursday practice, the twins got their first dose of good news in a while. Both safeties, Mark Zolla and Alister Edwards, were back on the field, the red spots on their faces already faded.

"Hey, Ronde," Tiki said, "now you can go back to your old position!"

"Yeah," Ronde said wistfully. "To tell you the truth, though, I was kind of enjoying safety."

"Yeah, and you could get used to playing quarterback, too, if they gave you a chance," Tiki said with a laugh.

"Hey, I can't help it if I'm a natural talent," Ronde shot back, grinning.

The bad news was that Sam Scarfone was still out. His return for the game was iffy at best. But at least having their safeties back was sure to improve the Eagle defense against a Charlottesville passing attack that was number one in the state.

As for the offense, they were clicking in practice like they hadn't in a long time—since before the whole chicken pox plague had first shown up. "They may be number one in passing," John Berra told Tiki, "but we've got the best running game in the state."

"My man!" Tiki said, and the two of them butted helmets.

Yes, it was going to be quite a game, Tiki thought. The two teams might even run up a higher score than in the Abingdon game.

Tiki's good mood lasted as long as he was on the field. But as soon as practice was over, that happy feeling started to fade. Every kid on the late bus wanted to talk to the twins about football. Tiki was glad when they finally got home and he could do his homework in peace.

He and Ronde spent the first part of the evening studying. Their mom was off at another community meeting, and once they finished their homework, they switched on the TV and watched an episode of *Star Trek*.

Their mom got home at nine, and brought a really good cheesecake with her. Both boys stuffed their faces—especially Tiki, who soon began to wish he hadn't eaten quite so much.

Soon it was bedtime, and Mrs. Barber shooed the boys

upstairs. "Big day tomorrow," she said. "You boys need to be well-rested for the big game."

"I can't wait for it to be over," Ronde confessed as he and Tiki got ready for bed.

"For *what* to be over?"

"You know—the game. *All* the games. The whole season."

"Don't say that, man—if it's over too quick, that means we lost!"

"No, I don't mean it like that," Ronde said. "I just mean . . ."

"I know—the pressure."

"Exactly."

"I hear you," Tiki said. His stomach was starting to feel really queasy now—so queasy that he was starting to sweat.

Ronde got washed up first—the bathroom was only big enough for one—and then it was Tiki's turn. He got inside, closed the door, and ran some cold water over his face.

Was he going to be okay? he wondered. Yes, he thought so. His stomach was calming down now, although he was still sweating. In fact, he was feeling suddenly cold. Shivering, he took a look in the bathroom mirror—

Oh, no!

He blinked hard, but the mirror image remained the same. His entire face, from forehead to chin, was covered with tiny dark spots!

Oh, nonononooooo!!!

He grabbed a wet washcloth and rubbed it hard over his face, trying to make the spots disappear. Trying to obliterate them, exterminate them, rub them into oblivion!

But the spots remained where they were. Tiki looked into the mirror, staring at the face of disaster. And suddenly, thinking of the big game coming up, he began to feel really, really sick.

CHAPTER EIGHT

A WALKING NIGHTMARE

RONDE HEARD THE DREADFUL GASP FROM THE bathroom, then the sound of water gushing out of the faucet, then Tiki's moaning and groaning.

He got up out of bed and scooted to the bathroom. Peeking in, he could not believe his eyes. *"Oh, no!"*

"Shhh!" Tiki warned. "Mom's downstairs."

"She can't hear us, she's got her music on the stereo."

"Anyway, keep it down, just in case."

"Geez!" Ronde said, half-whispering. "I can't *believe* this!"

"Me neither."

"This is *bad.*"

"*Really* bad," Tiki agreed.

"What are we gonna do now?"

"What do you mean, what are *we* gonna do?"

"I mean, you've got the chicken pox!"

Tiki rolled his eyes. "Duh. Don't you think I can see that? I've got eyes."

"Well?"

"Well, I don't know what to do!"

77

"Wait till Mom sees."

"She's not *gonna* see," Tiki shot back.

"What?"

"You heard me. And you're not gonna tell her!"

"She's gonna know, first thing in the morning."

"Well . . . I'll have to think of something by then," said Tiki.

"She's gonna want to take you to the doctor."

"I'm not going to any doctor."

"I don't know, Tiki. . . ."

"Just go back to bed, Ronde. You're not helping by staring at me like that."

Ronde had a lot more he wanted to say, but he thought better of it and got back into bed. Tiki shut the lights, yanked the cover over his head, and was silent.

Ronde listened to his own breathing in the dark room. He thought he heard his twin sniffing back tears, but he couldn't be sure.

And what if Tiki *was* crying under that blanket? Who could blame him?

Just think what it would be like to get sick and miss the biggest game of your life! Ronde almost felt like crying himself. He felt really bad for his brother, and even worse for the team! What would their chances be without Tiki on the field?

Worst of all, in his heart of hearts, Ronde couldn't help feeling relieved it wasn't *him* who had the spots.

And that was another thing—how come he didn't, and Tiki did?

Well, he reasoned, Tiki had spent a lot of time around Berra. They always hung around together at practice.

On the other hand, Ronde's locker was right next to Berra's, and he and Tiki were always together. Now that Tiki had come down with the dreaded spots, how long until Ronde got them too?

And *then* where would the Eagles be?

Ronde pulled his socks on so hard that he ripped one, and had to go hunt in his drawer for another pair. Of all the bad things that had happened to the Eagles this season, Tiki getting sick now was by far the worst. Why did the stupid chicken pox have to show up in Roanoke just when the Eagles' dream of a state championship was on the verge of coming true?

Ronde couldn't remember the last time he'd gone to school without Tiki. Usually, when one of them got a cold or a flu, the other got it at the same time. Now, he was going to have to be the one to break the bad news to everyone. He wished he could duck back under the covers and hide for the rest of the day.

But that was not going to happen. Mrs. Barber was already calling from downstairs that breakfast was ready, and that they'd better come down and eat it quick, or they'd miss the school bus.

Tiki was lying in bed, sweating bullets, shivering and miserable. "Tiki, I'm gonna have to tell Mom."

Tiki didn't answer.

"Tiki?"

Still nothing, except for a low moan.

"Okay, then. Bye." Ronde went downstairs and broke the news to his mom. She ran right up to see Tiki, and Ronde was left to eat his breakfast alone.

He wanted to kick something. He was furious. He would have gone ballistic, if he could have figured out whom to be mad at. "This is all Tiki's fault," he told himself as he ate. "Why did he have to go and get sick?"

But he knew Tiki couldn't help it, any more than Berra could have, or Sam, or the others who'd gone down with the virus. In fact, it was only dumb luck that Ronde had stayed healthy—so far.

As he rode the bus to school, he thought of his brother with pity instead. *Poor Tiki.* All the Eagles—even Sam Scarfone, he was sure—would be back on the field against Charlottesville West—all except Tiki.

His poor brother would lie in bed, helpless, while the Eagles fought for play-off survival. If they lost, everyone would blame Tiki for not being there. And if the team somehow managed to win, Tiki would have missed out on their most heroic victory yet! Either way, it was a bad break for him.

But who am I kidding? Ronde asked himself. Without

Tiki, the Eagles couldn't *possibly* win. He was their best player—at least on offense. Without him, Ronde figured, the defense would have to hold Charlottesville to zero points!

Yeah, right, Ronde thought. *Like that's ever gonna happen.* Charlottesville hadn't lost all season, and they were averaging over four touchdowns a game!

Ronde sighed, grabbed his bag, and followed the other kids off the bus and into school. This was going to be a terrible day. And nothing he or anybody else could do would make it one bit better.

"Hi, Ronde!" Adam greeted him just inside the entry-way. "Where's Tiki?"

Ronde gave him a look that needed no words.

"You're kidding! Please tell me you're kidding."

Ronde just stared at him.

"Oh, no!" Adam cried. "That stinks so bad! What are we gonna do now?"

Ronde shrugged his shoulders.

"What, do you not speak anymore?" Adam asked. "Laryngitis or something?"

"Ha, ha," Ronde said.

"He speaks! See that? I cured you. Too bad I don't know how to cure chicken pox."

Adam was usually funny, but Ronde wasn't laughing today. Nothing in the world would have made him crack a smile that morning.

By lunchtime, when the team gathered in the cafeteria, word had gotten around. Even the food servers behind the counter wore stricken looks on their faces. Tiki's being ill was a body blow to the whole school's hopes.

"Man, don't sit next to me," Paco told Ronde. "You might be contagious."

"Yeah, you're probably next," said Cody. "Go sit somewhere else, dude. Things are bad enough already."

Ronde realized Cody wasn't joking. They were all his friends, but he could see by their looks that none of them wanted to sit near him—not today, anyway.

Sadly, he went to look for an empty table. Finding one, he ate quickly, and got up to go spend the rest of the period in the playground.

But before he got outside, the school nurse stopped him. "Ronde?" she called, sticking her head outside the office door. "How are you feeling? I hear your brother is sick."

"Uh-huh. Chicken pox."

"Mm-hmm. And how are *you* feeling?"

Ronde shrugged. "I'm not sick, but I feel bad."

"Oh, I know exactly what you mean. You poor thing," she said, putting a hand on his shoulder. "I hate to say this, but I'm going to have to ask you to go home."

Ronde snapped to attention. "Say what?"

"I know you're not sick—yet—but the fact that you

live with someone who *is* means you could be carry-ing the virus and exposing others, even before you have any symptoms. So I'd like you to stay home until your brother is past the infection stage and you're past the incubation period."

"Huh?"

"For a few days, anyway. I'll arrange for your teachers to call your mother and give them work for you to do at home, but I don't want to risk a general epidemic in the school."

"But—"

"I'm really sorry, Ronde, believe me. It's the last thing I want to do. But I've got to think of the other students' health."

He could see she wasn't going to back down. "Okay, whatever. But what about the big game?"

The nurse thought for a moment. "Well, that's not for a few days yet. If you're still well by then, I suppose I could allow you to play. But no practices before that."

"*No practices*? But—"

"I'm sorry, Ronde. We've already had enough mem-bers of the team get sick. We can't afford any more."

"But if we lose this game, it'll all be over, and then it doesn't matter who gets sick."

"I beg your pardon? Doesn't matter? When children miss school, it matters very much."

"Then why do I have to go home?"

"Ronde, I know how you feel, but this is important. There are certain children with other, more serious health conditions, and for them, catching chicken pox could be very dangerous. I have to insist. I'm sorry."

Just then, a girl approached them, holding her stomach and looking distinctly green. "Mrs. Davis," she said to the nurse, "I feel sick . . ."

"Oh, my goodness," said the nurse. "Come on, Maria, let's get you to the bathroom right away." She began leading the girl out, then turned back to Ronde.

"Wait in the main office, Ronde. I'll phone your mother and—"

"She's at work."

"Oh, I see," said the nurse. "Well, then, I'll call the emergency contact and have them come drive you home."

There was no way to argue, because the nurse quickly left with Maria for the girls' room. Ronde sat in the main office, reading magazines and twiddling his thumbs. He had to wait over half an hour until their neighbor, Mrs. Prendergast, picked him up in her old jalopy and drove him home.

Tiki was surprised to see him, but Ronde quickly explained.

"Cool," Tiki said. "Now at least I'll have some company. It's boring being alone here all day."

"Not cool," Ronde replied. "I'm not even sick, and

the school nurse makes me go home. Now I'm gonna fall behind in all my subjects!"

"What do you think is gonna happen to *me*?"

"Same thing, I guess."

"Well, we could help each other study," Tiki pointed out. "We've got lots of time—all week, in fact."

Ronde sighed deeply. Usually, he'd be glad to have a day or two off from school. But not this week. Now, he'd have to hang around the house with Tiki, whose spotted face was a constant reminder that any minute, Ronde too might get sick, and have to miss the biggest game of his life!

CHAPTER NINE
MIRACLE CURE

TIKI TOSSED AND TURNED IN BED, UNABLE TO FALL asleep. It wasn't just the unbearable itching—although he was sure that without it, he'd be asleep by now. It was the thought of missing the Charlottesville game that was keeping him awake.

From the other side of the room, he could hear Ronde's regular breathing. Obviously, the tension wasn't bad enough to keep *him* awake.

Tiki stared at the alarm clock as the numbers slowly flipped the minutes away. 2:33 . . . 2:34 . . . 2:35 . . .

He didn't know exactly how long it took for chicken pox to go away. But he knew he wasn't going to be able to play this week's game against the Raiders. If the Eagles lost, everyone would say it was his fault. He *couldn't* let that go down. It was eating at him already, and it hadn't even happened yet!

Ronde was snoring softly. For a moment, Tiki allowed himself to imagine what would have happened if it had been *Ronde* who'd gotten sick instead. He figured it would have been just as bad for the Eagles. But of course, it would have been *him* snoring right now, and Ronde itching but forbidden to scratch.

"Don't touch your spots!" their mom had warned him. "You'll get scars!" Tiki worried about that. He didn't want to get scars—but it was almost impossible *not* to scratch!

He remembered the time, a few years back, when their cousin Melvin had come down with chicken pox. Tiki and Ronde hadn't been allowed anywhere near him, but when they finally did see Melvin—from a safe distance—they'd both laughed at how funny he looked with all those spots.

Well, Tiki wasn't laughing now. When you were a member of the Hidden Valley Eagles, everything was different. You were representing your whole school— teachers, students, janitors—*everybody. Nobody* was laughing about Tiki's chicken pox, least of all Ronde.

Tiki's twin was tossing and turning now in his sleep. *Having bad dreams*, Tiki guessed. *He thinks he's next.*

Tiki looked at the alarm clock again: 3:11. Was he going to go the whole night without a wink of sleep? The itching was driving him crazy! He kept his hands at his side, but it was really, really hard not to scratch.

This was so unfair! The Eagles were only two wins away from being state champions—the best team in the whole state of Virginia, home of George Washington, Thomas Jefferson, and . . . and . . . Tiki and Ronde Barber. . . .

Suddenly, Ronde awoke with a start. *"Aaah!"* he cried out softly, sitting up and blinking his sleepy eyes. "What happened?" He looked around the darkened room, confused.

"Go back to sleep, dude," Tiki told him. "You were dreaming."

Ronde blew out a relieved breath. "Whoa," he said, then yawned. "I was being chased by a bunch of spotted eagles that wanted to peck me with their beaks."

"Nightmare," Tiki said.

"You got that right."

"Go back to sleep, Ronde."

"Okay." And just like that, he lay down again, and was out like a light.

Tiki shook his head and smiled. Ronde never did have any problem falling asleep. All he had to do was put his head on the pillow and close his eyes.

Tiki usually slept just as well, but not this week. Not tonight.

Again, he found himself pained by the unfairness of it all. After all the hard work he'd done in practice, all the pounding he'd taken during the games . . . After having to be the team's kicker when Adam got suspended . . . After a whole seventh-grade season of sitting on the bench while the team won the district championship without him. All of that waiting, suffering, and doing battle on the field, just to get to this moment.

And now, to have it snatched away from him, just like that, by a stroke of pure bad luck?

No! No way! He just couldn't take it!

He *had* to play this weekend, he just had to.

Hadn't their mom always told them, "Don't ever give up, boys. You never have to take things lying down. There's always something you can do to make things better, for yourself and for everybody else."

She was right! Why should he take this bad break lying down? He sat up in bed and madly tapped his feet on the floor as he wracked his brain for an idea—some way of getting around this terrible thing that had happened to him. . . .

He felt his forehead—not too warm. His fever was already starting to go down. And he didn't feel like hurling any more. So that part was okay. Maybe he could just tell everyone he was all better.

But those stupid, stupid spots! There they were, all over his face, chest, back, arms, and legs, for everyone to see. And nothing he could do would make them disappear in time to play the game. Nothing he could ever do, no future success on the football field, would make up for this terrible blow. Nothing could make up for . . . make up for . . .

"*Makeup!*" he cried, slapping his hands together. "That's it!"

Ronde snorted and opened his eyes. "Huh? What did you say?"

"Nothing. Go back to sleep."

And Ronde did, instantly. Tiki smiled and shook his head. By the time Ronde woke up on Saturday morning, Tiki was going to be all better—or at least, he was going to *look* that way!

The next day, while Mrs. Barber was at work and Ronde was busy watching TV, Tiki snuck up to his mom's bathroom and opened her makeup drawer. He took out something called foundation, and tried sponging it onto a few of the spots on his face.

Then he checked himself out in the mirror. The makeup covered the spots pretty well—not completely, of course, but enough so that they looked like they were healing.

If Coach, and his mom, and everyone else saw him now, they'd think he was well enough to play, Tiki decided. Never mind that his recovery was too quick to be believable—he would deal with that, somehow, when the time came.

For now, he just pocketed the foundation and the sponge and hid them under his own mattress. His mom had so many others she'd never miss it. And on Saturday morning, he'd get up early, before anyone else, and perform a miracle cure that would get him into the big game!

Afterward, he might have to deal with people yelling at him for exposing them to chicken pox, maybe even making fun of him for wearing makeup. But he could take all the abuse, all the ridicule, if it meant he could play against Charlottesville West, and maybe win the big game for Hidden Valley.

He was sure he'd be punished somehow, if—no, *when*—his fakery was unmasked. But he didn't care. All he cared about was winning the game, and after that, the state championship.

By Friday night, Tiki's fever was long gone. His itching had calmed down some, but he still had scabs on his spots, and there was no way anyone would let him play tomorrow—not without his little "miracle cure," that is.

He didn't set his alarm. It would have awakened Ronde and blown the whole scheme. Instead, Tiki simply forced himself to get up early—so early it was still dark outside.

Ronde was fast asleep. So was their mom, who was able to sleep because she had to take one day off from work today. This morning she'd be driving Ronde to the bus, and then follow along with the caravan of moms, dads, brothers, sisters, fellow students, teachers, and other fans of the Eagles, all making the long trip to Charlottesville to watch the biggest game their team had ever played.

Tiki reached under his mattress and brought out the tin of foundation and the sponge. Then he tiptoed into the bathroom, and softly shut the door behind him before flipping the light switch.

Yep. The spots were still there, all right. Better, but not better enough. He opened the tin, and one by one, covered the spots with just enough makeup to look natural. It took a long time, because the spots were pretty much everywhere. Then he had to blend it all in so it wasn't noticeable. At least, not very.

Did he look natural enough to fool people? He thought so. In this light, at least, he seemed almost all better, and certainly not bad enough to be contagious.

Good. Now to get back in bed and pretend to sleep. He shoved the tin and the sponge under his pillow and closed his eyes.

He drifted off to sleep once or twice, but not for very long. Soon he heard his mom moving around in her room. Then she went downstairs, and five minutes later, she called the boys down to breakfast.

Tiki stayed in bed until Ronde had gone downstairs. Then he quickly got dressed—in street clothes, not the pajamas he'd been wearing all week.

"Mom!" he cried. "Mom! Ronde! Check this out—*I'm better*!" He waited as the two of them ran upstairs to see what he was talking about.

"Whoa!" Ronde said, breaking into a huge smile at the sight of his brother's face. "You really *do* look better! Can you play in the game?"

"Can dogs bark at mailmen?" Tiki replied, and the two boys slapped five.

Their mom, however, seemed to hold back a little.

"Hmmm," she said, checking Tiki out closely—a little *too* closely for comfort, Tiki thought. "That really *is* amazing."

"It is, isn't it?" Tiki said excitedly.

"Unbelievable," she said. "I never heard of anyone getting over chicken pox this fast."

"It's a miracle!" Tiki told her. "Now I can play today!"

"Hmmm . . ."

"I knew I was getting better last night when I—what are you doing, Ma?"

She was bending over the bed, examining his pillow. *Uh-oh.*

"What is this brown stain on my nice white pillowcase?" she asked, frowning. She picked up the pillow, and discovered the makeup and sponge hidden beneath. "Tiki Barber, what in the world have you been up to?"

"Um, me? Nothing."

"Don't lie to me, now."

"I . . ."

She took a hanky from her pocket and wiped his face. Makeup came off on it, revealing Tiki's "miracle cure" for the fraud it was.

Tiki was stuck. Nailed. Way busted. There was no way out now but to tell the awful truth.

93

So that's what he did. His mother listened sympatheti-cally, but Ronde burst out laughing.

"Ha! Tiki wears makeup! I can't believe this—man, you are gonna be the laughingstock of the whole team. No, the whole school!"

"No, I'm not. Because you're not going to say a word about it."

"Oh, I don't know about that," Ronde said, laughing again.

"You'd better keep your mouth shut!" Tiki shouted, jumping on Ronde and wrestling him to the ground. Ronde kept laughing, but to Tiki, it was anything but funny to think that everyone would know how low he'd sunk to get himself on the field.

"Stop laughing!" Tiki ordered.

"I can't!" Ronde said, even as Tiki sat on top of him, holding his arm behind his back.

"Ow! Ha-ha! Ow!"

"Tiki, stop that right now!" Mrs. Barber ordered, in a tone of voice that stopped both boys in their tracks. "Get off your brother."

Tiki slowly got off. "It's not funny," he said. "I only did it for the team."

"I know you did, baby," his mom said, hugging him. "But it won't help the team if you show up and play at half-strength."

"I know," Tiki mumbled. "But—"

"Did you ever hear of Typhoid Mary?" she asked him.

"Typhoid who?"

"She made a whole town sick, with a disease a lot worse than chicken pox. I know how much you want to win, baby. But your health, and everybody else's, is even more important than winning. Don't be a Typhoid Mary."

"Aw, Ma," Tiki said. "It's only chicken pox."

"I'm not going to argue with you anymore," she said flatly. "Except to say that even if you played today, and the Eagles won, how are they gonna win the championship game next week if you make half the team sick?"

Tiki had no answer. There was none.

"And Ronde," Mrs. Barber went on, "put yourself in your brother's shoes. Would you have done any different?"

Ronde's smile vanished. The thought of being in Tiki's shoes was not funny at all.

"Tiki's right," she continued. "Don't you say a word about this to anybody. Ever. You hear?"

"Yes, Ma," Ronde said, looking at the floor, then back up at Tiki. "Don't worry, bro," he said. "I'm gonna personally make sure you get to be in another game this season, and *you* can win *that* one for us. Okay?"

"That's a deal," Tiki said, fighting back tears. "Go get 'em, Ronde. Win this one for me. Keep our season alive till I can get back."

"Count on it."

Ronde and Tiki gave each other their secret hand-shake—the one only the two of them knew, and that they used only at their most special moments. "We're gonna win this one," Ronde said. "I guarantee it."

CHAPTER TEN

YOU WILL NOT LET THEM PASS

NOW, WHY DID I GO AND OPEN MY BIG MOUTH? Ronde wondered. He'd guaranteed his twin a victory. *Guaranteed* it. As if any one player on a fifty-man football team could guarantee anything.

Nevertheless, he'd promised, and now it was up to him to deliver somehow.

Ronde figured that the Charlottesville West Raiders would be hard to beat. They'd gone undefeated all season, and were considered the favorites—except, of course, in Roanoke—to win the state championship. In fact, most of their victories had been lopsided, if not embarrassing, for the losing teams. This Ronde knew from studying their season box scores, which had been posted in that week's *Roanoke Reporter.*

Ronde also noticed that in their few close games, the Raiders hadn't scored much. They'd won by holding their opponents to no more than three points.

That told Ronde that their defense was better than their offense. He figured that without Tiki, the Eagles would have a hard time scoring points. That left them only one way to win—he, and the rest of the defense, would have to hold the Raiders scoreless, or pretty close to it, anyway.

It didn't help that the game was being played in Charlottesville, a two-hour bus ride away. The Raiders' bleachers and field seats were all stacked with their fans, yelling and screaming and hoisting signs and pom-poms and banners in the air. The Eagles fans were making as much noise as they could, but they were hopelessly out-numbered, and they were drowned out by the wall of noise from the amped-up Raiders crowd.

Ronde was back at cornerback today, covering the Raiders' star receiver, Shadeik Stratford. Stratford was number one in the state in receptions, touchdowns, yard-age, and every other measurement known to man.

No, this was not going to be easy. But Ronde had made a promise, and he intended to keep it.

The Eagles got the ball first, and Cody, following Coach Wheeler's game plan, tried to keep it on the ground, going to John Berra and Luke Frazier in Tiki's absence. Neither of them was used to carrying the ball very much. They did manage a couple of first downs and ate up a lot of time on the clock, which was a big part of Coach Wheeler's plan. He figured that the less time the Raiders had the ball, the better.

When the drive stalled, Adam punted it a long way, pinning the Raiders deep in their own end. From there, they too had to run the ball, and Ronde knew it. He left his man to the safeties, and darted over to join Sam Scarfone in stuffing the run. Sam was still weak from his bout with chicken pox, and he needed all the help he could get. With Ronde backing him up, the defense forced the Raiders to punt.

Ronde ran it back to near midfield, and once again, the Eagles had the ball. They stayed on the ground, even though it soon became clear they weren't going to get very far that way. Finally, Adam tried a long field goal that missed.

Now, with the first quarter almost over, the Raiders got to work for real. The first pass that came Stratford's way was a post pattern. The receiver didn't even bother to fake Ronde out, figuring he could just outrun him. But Ronde, small though he was, was every bit as fast as Stratford. Not only did he keep up with him, he beat him to the ball, and came down with a spectacular interception!

"That's for Tiki!" he yelled to the booing crowd, holding the ball up for them to see whose it was now.

Coach Wheeler doggedly kept the Eagles on the ground, eating up the clock. Finally he let Cody loose, and the quarterback found Fred Soule for a long gain, into Raider territory. Then it was back to the running game, until Adam nailed a short field goal, and the Eagles took a 3–0 lead.

If only the final gun would sound right now! Ronde thought. He knew how lucky he'd been to take the Raiders by surprise with his speed. Surely next time, the QB would throw it high, where only Stratford could grab it.

That's exactly what happened on third down. Ronde knew he couldn't jump as high as Stratford, so he timed his leap for when the receiver was coming back down. With his arm thrust skyward, Ronde knocked the ball loose before the completion was made! Once again, the Raiders had to punt.

Ronde could sense the other team's frustration. He knew they'd be coming after this punt big-time. So when he caught the ball, he waited an extra second to let them get really close—then took off, darting straight forward, splitting two defenders before they knew what was happening.

By the time he was brought down, he was in Raider territory again. Unfortunately, this time the Eagle running game went exactly nowhere. The only good thing was, they managed to eat up enough time so that the first half ended before Charlottesville could mount another drive, keeping Hidden Valley ahead, 3–0.

"I'll take it, I'll take it!" Coach Wheeler said with a smile as he welcomed the team back into the visitors' locker room at halftime. "Way to go, Ronde! What a first half!"

He high-fived Ronde, who also accepted the backslaps and helmet smacks that were raining down on him.

"Take it easy!" he complained. "The game's not over yet!"

"Exactly!" Coach Wheeler said. "Guys, this second half is going to be the toughest thirty minutes you've ever played. Cody, we're going to go play-action on our first drive—see if we can sucker them in. Defense, we'll be running a lot of blitzes. Let's see if we can rattle their cage a little. I don't think they've been behind at the half all year."

"They haven't," Ronde confirmed. He knew that much from the box scores. He also knew what the Raiders must feel like in their locker room right now. They would be nervous, maybe even a little uptight. If the Eagles could score on them again, and put them in a hole, the mighty Raiders might just start making dumb mistakes.

Ronde suddenly felt dizzy. He'd been running his head off the whole first half, and now he needed to sit down. Grabbing a drink and downing it in two big gulps, he found an empty bench and lay down on it. After a couple minutes, he still didn't feel like himself, so he went into the bathroom to throw some cold water on his face.

He took off his helmet and turned on the faucet. Then he saw himself in the mirror—and froze.

SPOTS! There were spots breaking out all over his face!

No. Nononono! This cannot be happening, he thought.

"Ronde? You in there?"

Ronde jammed his helmet back on before anyone could see the state he was in. "Yeah?"

It was Adam. "Second half's about to start. You ready?"

"Ready as I'll ever be," Ronde told him, as if nothing was wrong. As if nothing had changed.

Funny . . . he hadn't felt sick until just the moment before. Or maybe he *had* felt sick all day, and just put it down to nervousness. Either way, now he was going to have to tough it out, playing through the second half without ever taking off his helmet.

Later, after the game, he would act as surprised as everyone else. For now, there was no chicken pox, no spots—there was nothing but the game . . . and his solemn promise to Tiki.

The second half began with Adam kicking off. Ronde raced down the field, heading straight for Shadeik Stratford, who, in addition to being the Raiders' top receiver, also ran back kickoffs. Ronde got to him just after the ball did. He grabbed Stratford around the legs, and although the big receiver shook him off, the delay was fatal. Stratford went down under a pile of Eagles.

The Raiders were back in their own end again, but this time, they worked their short passing game to perfection, staying away from Stratford—and Ronde. Good thing, too, because Ronde was still feeling weird—he couldn't decide whether he was hot or cold, and every once in a while, a wave of queasiness would rise in his stomach, and he'd have to force it back down.

Luckily, the Eagle linebackers were on their game, and

held the Raider gains to a minimum. Still, seven minutes later, Charlottesville West was knocking at the door, parked in the red zone on the Eagle three, with third and goal to go.

Coach Wheeler called a safety blitz. Ronde's job was to stick with his man, just in case the Raider QB got free, or managed to get the pass off before he was tackled.

The blitz was successful—so successful that the quarterback, tackled from behind, fumbled the ball. It bounced around, then got kicked forward into the end zone!

Ronde, who'd been trailing his man, sticking to him like a barnacle, saw the ball bounce toward him. He leaped toward it, and so did Stratford. The two boys wrestled for it madly, but Ronde had his body between Stratford and the ball, and came away with it. He held onto it for dear life as players from both teams piled on.

Hands tried clawing it away from him, but Ronde just kept thinking of his promise to Tiki. Nothing, and no one, was going to get that ball away from him!

"Touchback! Eagle ball!" called the referee. The whistle blew, the pile got off Ronde. He stood up, breathless, nauseous, shivering—and handed the ball to the ref.

"Nice play, little guy," said the ref, and patted him on the helmet.

Now why did he have to go and say that? Ronde wondered, shaking his head. He hated being small. *Hated* it.

Still, he'd made the play of the game so far, and saved his team a touchdown. He headed back to the bench to rest, hoping to somehow shake off the sickness that was making him feel worse and worse every minute.

The Eagles still had the lead, and the ball, too. But they were deep in their own end, and time was running short. Now the Raider defense began to show why it was number one in the state. They sacked Cody back at the ten yard line. Then they sacked him again at the five. And on third down, they blitzed him so hard that he had to throw the ball away.

It was only Adam Costa and his magic kicking foot that saved them. Adam booted the longest punt of his life, sending the ball way, way downfield. With the lucky bounce it took, the ball wound up at the Raider forty-yard line—a fifty-five yard kick!

By now, it was clear that this game was going to be won by the team that scored last. Ronde, sick as he was, was determined to preserve the shutout.

The Raiders ran the ball for a few plays in a row, driving forward to midfield and a first down. Then, a pass interference call on Mark Zolla brought Charlottesville West to the Eagle thirty. The third quarter ended, and the teams switched ends of the field.

"Barber!" Coach Pellugi called him over. Putting an arm around Ronde, he said, "Listen, they're bound to throw your way any play now. You've got to stay right up in your man's face, right from scrimmage. Got it?"

"Uh-huh."

"And give him a hard bump coming off the line."

"Right."

"And no penalties!"

"Got it, Coach."

"And Ronde?"

"Yes, Coach?" Ronde froze, wondering if Coach Pellugi had noticed something wrong with him—or worse, spotted his spots!

Pellugi paused for a moment. Then he said, "Good luck, kid. This is it. This is your moment. Make it happen."

Ronde nodded. He knew it was true. All his life, he'd practiced hard, working to improve his skills, to get stronger, faster, tougher, smarter. Now, everything was riding on this next fifteen minutes. If they won, they would go on to Richmond to play one final game for the state championship.

If they lost . . .

No. No, they were not going to lose. Ronde had guaranteed it, and it was up to him to make good, even if they had to cart him off to the doctor afterward. Clapping his hands, he ran back out onto the field.

The teams lined up. The ball was snapped. Ronde smashed head-on into Stratford as he came off the line, causing him to stumble. While he tried to regain his balance, the Eagle blitz rained down on the Raiders' quarterback, forcing him to throw the ball away.

Ronde bent over double in the defensive huddle, trying to make the nausea settle down.

"Hey, Barber, you okay?" Sam asked him.

Ronde nodded.

Sam stared at him, squinting. Then he nodded slowly, as if he knew, and understood. "Hang in there, dude. You're doing awesome."

Ronde couldn't manage an answer, but it didn't matter. The defense clapped hands once and headed back to battle. Next time the Raiders went to Stratford, Ronde felt sure the receiver would deke to make him miss the bump. Well, whatever Stratford tried, Ronde would be ready.

The Raiders play-faked, then passed over the middle to their running back. Ronde left his man to make the tackle in the open field, but not before Charlottesville got another first down. They were at the twenty now, in the Eagles' red zone again.

This was the game, right here, Ronde knew. He wanted so badly just to lie down—but he couldn't; not yet.

After two running plays got the ball down to the Eagle thirteen, it was third and three. Time for another pass play, Ronde figured. Knowing that the Eagle safeties were backed up in the end zone, Ronde played right up on the line of scrimmage, making Stratford think he was going to try and bump him again.

Stratford deked, but Ronde didn't bite on the fake. He stayed right with his man as the Eagles' pass rush forced the QB from the pocket. He rolled right, toward Ronde and his man. Now Ronde had a choice—should he release Stratford and go after the quarterback? Or should he stick to Stratford no matter what?

There was no time to decide. Ronde did what his instincts told him to. He took one step toward the quarterback, pretending to rush him. Then, as the QB reached back to throw the ball over his head, Ronde backed off again, tracking the ball until he ran it down. Just as Stratford was about to grab it, Ronde flicked out his hand and deflected the ball—right into the hands of Sam Scarfone!

Sam looked like he'd just been handed a baby space alien. Then, he realized he had the ball, and fell to the ground, covering it with his massive bulk.

Eagle ball!

Now, Cody Hansen showed why Coach Wheeler had shown so much patience and confidence in him all season. Under ferocious pressure, he stood his ground, nailing his receivers for three short passes up the middle. They netted three straight first downs, bringing the Eagles out of their own red zone, and all the way up near midfield.

Ronde, catching his breath and trying not to lose his lunch, sat on the bench and looked up at the clock. Five minutes left. *He couldn't wait for this game to end!*

But could his team hold on to the ball long enough to ice the game, or would he have to get back out there, with his last ounce of strength, and do battle once more?

The Eagles were back to the ground game now, eating up precious seconds with every play. Three times the Raiders called time-out, but three was all they had. With two minutes left, Adam Costa came out onto the field and notched his second field goal of the game.

Now it was 6–0, Eagles. The Raiders would need a touchdown, not just a field goal, to take back the game. Ronde lined up with the kicking team, determined to use his last reserves of energy to stop any runback in its tracks.

The kick was high and deep. Ronde pushed the nausea out of his mind, ignored the pounding of his head and the cold sweat running down his face, and hurtled down the field at warp speed.

Shadeik Stratford looked down at the last minute, sensing Ronde coming at him. By the time he looked back up, he'd lost sight of the ball! It hit off his helmet and bounced away, with players from both teams racing after it.

Unfortunately, one of the Raiders covered it. The good news was, there hadn't been any runback. Now Charlottesville West would have to march seventy yards in ninety seconds to win the game.

Ronde knew what that meant. They'd be throwing deep, to their number one receiver. Which meant that the entire outcome of the game was in his hands.

Just where he wanted it.

Sick as he felt, he wouldn't have had it any other way. This was his moment, and no stupid chicken pox was going to steal it from him!

Stratford stared hard at him. He seemed to sense Ronde's weakness, and a look came into his eyes—the look of a tiger about to pounce.

Ronde thought one last time of his promise to Tiki.

The snap came, and Stratford took off. Ronde didn't bother to hit him—he was too weak for that anyway. He just kept stride for stride with the receiver, and when Stratford made his move, Ronde was ready. He stepped between Stratford and the pass, gathered himself, and leaped as high as he could, reaching . . . reaching . . .

. . . and came down with the football!

The Eagles swarmed out onto the field to mob him, but Ronde was too quick for them. He sprinted to the sidelines, and removed his helmet just before his teammates reached him.

"WHOA!" several of them said at once. "Barber— you've got—"

"Don't tell me, let me guess," said Ronde, exhausted but happy. "Chicken pox?"

"Dude, how long have you known?" asked Cody.

"Me?" Ronde replied, his eyes wide with innocence. "I had no idea till you all just told me."

Out on the field, the final gun sounded. The game was over. The Eagles were in the state championship game!

The other kids mobbed each other, dancing up and down and chanting "Ea-gles! Ea-gles!" All except Ronde. He sat alone on the bench, the player of the game, the one guy all of them would have wanted most to hug and hoist on their shoulders—if only they dared come near him!

He was now officially on the sick list. He knew that meant big trouble going forward—but for now, he didn't even want to think about that. He lay back, shivering with chills, itching all over, sick to his stomach, and as happy as he'd ever felt in his life.

A promise made, a promise kept. It had been a foolish thing to do, but he was glad he'd done it. If he hadn't, there was no way the Eagles would have pulled off this improbable victory without Tiki's help.

The question now was—would Tiki have to do the same for him in the state finals?

CHAPTER ELEVEN

STEP UP

FOR TIKI, THE WAIT HAD BEEN UNBEARABLE.
All that morning and early afternoon, he paced the floor, drummed his fingers on the table, tap-tapped with his homework pencil, and tried unsuccessfully to forget everything by watching TV. Seeing the Cavaliers of Virginia beat up on the Hokies of Virginia Tech only reminded Tiki of that other huge game going on at the same time over in Charlottesville.

It was late in the afternoon when the door banged open and Tiki heard Ronde let out a whoop. "TIKIIII!!"

Tiki ran from the kitchen to the living room, a jar of mayonnaise still in his hand. Ronde had caught him in the middle of making a sandwich, but this was definitely more important. "What happened?" Tiki shouted, but he already knew, from the happy tone of his twin's voice.

"VICTORY!" Ronde yelled, throwing his hands high as Tiki burst into the room.

"WOO-HOO!" Tiki ran to hug his brother, but stopped just short when he saw Ronde's face. "What in the—?"

"That's right, bro," Ronde said with a smile and a

111

shake of the head. "I didn't know it was coming on till halftime."

"Did they make you leave the game?"

Ronde made a face that meant *Are you crazy?* and said, "No, man—I kept my helmet jammed on so nobody could see! I wasn't gonna get myself yanked from that game!"

"What was the score?"

"Ha! Six–zip, can you believe it?"

"What?"

"That's right, give it up," Ronde said, nodding and strutting, doing a little victory dance. "Oh, yeah, that's what I'm talkin' about. Shutout city, and yours truly had two picks and a sack, in case you were wondering."

"I can't believe it!" Tiki said. "Hey, don't scratch your spots—you'll get scars."

"I'm not! I'm just feeling them."

"Well, don't."

"You should talk—you've been scratching all week."

"Have not."

"Have too!"

"Aw, let's not get started on that," Tiki said. Blowing out a relieved sigh, he said, "I can't believe this—we really won!"

"I know you thought we'd fold without you. I *told* you we were gonna win this game. Didn't I? Come on, admit it!"

"It's true, it's true," Tiki said, grinning and shaking his head in disbelief. "Man, I am so relieved!"

"I can believe it."

"But—"

"But what?"

Tiki gestured toward Ronde's spot-covered face. "What are we gonna do *now?*"

"Hey, don't be bringing me down, dude," Ronde said, breezing past him and jumping over the back of the couch to lie down at last. "I'm still riding that beautiful wave."

"Sheesh!" Tiki said, laughing.

Their mom came in, shaking her head as she saw her two sons, both spotted like leopards. "What am I gonna do with you boys?"

Tiki knew she was as happy as they were. She'd lived this whole crazy season with them, sharing their ups and downs, giving them lots of encouragement at key moments, and a kick in the rear when they really needed it.

But she had to be tired. After six straight days at two different jobs, she could now rest for thirty-six hours before heading back to work. Except for the fact that she would have to cook, clean, and take care of her two itchy, pox-ridden sons, getting them to the doctor's and making sure they didn't scratch their spots.

Tiki took a seat in the easy chair across from Ronde and flicked the TV back on. Virginia Tech had come back, and was now making it close against Virginia. While their mom made dinner, Tiki lay there, thinking about the future.

His chicken pox were on the mend. Surely, he'd be able to play in the state championship, thanks to Ronde and the rest of the Eagles, and the great game they'd just won.

But what about Ronde? His chicken pox were just coming on! Although there was plenty of time yet before their ultimate game, Tiki knew Ronde would probably not be able to play. Unless he recovered faster than everyone else had, he wouldn't be ready in time.

The Eagles had won without Tiki. Could they win without Ronde? If they didn't, it would be awful! Losing the championship would be bad enough, after all they'd gone through to get this far. But losing it *because of Ronde getting sick* would be even worse!

"How you feeling?" Tiki asked him.

"Uugghhh. Bad. I probably shouldn't have been playing." He managed a smile. "How're you feeling yourself?"

"Better every day. I might even be able to practice by Monday."

"Good."

"I'll bring you your homework every day," Tiki promised.

"Yeah, I guess they'll let you go to school even though I'm sick."

"'Course they will. I've already had it. You can't get it twice."

"Right."

"Hey, Ronde?"

"Yeah?"

"You gonna be able to play?"

There was a long silence. Finally, Ronde said, "You'd best believe I'm gonna play."

"But what if you're not better by then?"

Another silence. Then, "I'll think of something. . . ."

"Well," came their mom's voice from the doorway, "it had better not involve my makeup."

"Mom!"

"Because my stuff is strictly off-limits from now on. Understood? Or do I have to put it under lock and key?"

"Mom!"

"All right then," she said, smiling before walking back into the room. "Come on, you two—dinner's ready."

"Smells good!" Tiki said.

"Ugh, I'm not hungry," Ronde said.

"Come on now—it's mac and cheese—your favorite. Fit for a couple of champions!"

Tiki and Ronde exchanged a happy look—but it faded quickly. They both knew the truth—in spite of everything, they weren't champions yet. And unless Ronde played in the big game, they might never be!

• • •

That week's *Roanoke Reporter* ran a full section of articles about the Hidden Valley Eagles and their amazing season. The lead article was about their chances in the upcoming state final versus the Fredericksburg Falcons.

"'Fredericksburg is a team that has not trailed in any of its games since late September,'" Tiki read. "'They blew away the competition in the East, while Hidden Valley had to battle a number of problems to get this far.'"

Below the lead article was a long recap of the Eagles' troubled season, detailing all the many obstacles they'd overcome on their way to this chance at everlasting glory. "'Even now, the team is weakened by an epidemic of chicken pox that has affected some of its key players at the worst possible moment,'" Tiki read. "Man, they sure got that right."

On the next page, there was a box score of each of the Eagles' games, along with an interview with Coach Wheeler, together with his assistants, Pete Pellugi and Steve Ontkos.

There were even profiles of some team members. One was of Cody Hansen. The quarterback is, after all, the on-field leader of any football team. There was also a story about Adam Costa, who had come out of nowhere the year before to emerge as the best kicker in the state. And finally, there was a big feature about Tiki and Ronde Barber, identical twin all-stars, one on offense and the other on defense.

"Hey, where'd they get these dumb pictures of us?" Ronde wondered, making a face.

"I think those are our sixth-grade school pictures," Tiki said.

"Right! That's why we look like little kids!"

"I don't think mine looks so bad," Tiki said, teasing. "Yours, though—eeuw."

"Shut up!"

"Ha!"

They were sitting at the breakfast table, wolfing down the eggs their mom had made them before taking off for work. Tiki had about five minutes before he had to run for the school bus.

Ronde, though, was still house-bound. His spots were at their peak, and the only thing that cheered him up was the hope that they would go away before Saturday afternoon's big game in Richmond.

"'Somehow, the Eagles managed to win without Tiki Barber, their star running back,'" Tiki read on. "'The victory was largely due to the heroics of Ronde Barber on pass defense. Rumor has it that Tiki has now passed the chicken pox to his twin, who will have to miss the championship game. Can Tiki step it up and score enough touchdowns to make up for the loss of his brother? Only time will tell, but these must be nervous times in the Barber house.'" Tiki looked up. "Right again."

"Ha. No pressure, though."

Tiki chuckled. "Don't worry, yo. I've got this handled. Trust me."

"What are you gonna do, switch uniforms back and forth and pretend to be both of us?"

"You think I couldn't do it?"

"I think you couldn't *get away* with it," Ronde corrected him.

"Mm, probably not. Anyway, you stepped up for me, so I'm gonna do the same for you."

"You're not gonna have to," Ronde insisted. "I'm gonna play in the game."

"You hope so."

"I *know* so."

"What do you mean, you know so? *How* do you know? Can you see the future?"

"Dude, I just *know*," Ronde insisted. "I'm gonna beat this thing in record time."

"Well," said Tiki, gathering up his book bag and taking his dishes to the sink, "I wish you luck." He paused at the back door. "No—I wish us *all* luck."

When the team left for Richmond on a pair of buses that Friday morning—one for the players, the other for the band and cheerleaders—Ronde was not with them. He was much better—his spots were less obvious, and his fever was gone—but he was still a couple of days away from not being contagious, and being able to play football.

The team, the band, and the cheerleaders had all been given the day off from school to make this trip, and they were super-excited—all except for Tiki. Without Ronde on this journey with him, he felt incomplete, like he was missing a part of himself.

Mrs. Barber drove Tiki to the school parking lot and waved good-bye as the bus pulled out. She had originally planned to travel with the team—several parents were being chaperones, which gave them the chance to be there in the state capital when their Eagles fought for glory.

Mrs. Barber had even arranged to take Friday and Saturday off from work—but now, of course, with Ronde staying behind, her coming to Richmond was out of the question. She would stay home with her sick child instead.

The mood on the bus was lighthearted, all the kids joking with one another, singing funny songs, and seeing who could make the grossest noises. Unlike in school or at practice, Mr. Wheeler and the other coaches seemed to be okay with a certain amount of fooling around.

Still, Tiki knew that underneath all the goofiness, there was a shadow hanging over the team. Five or six players, including Tiki, still had red areas on their faces and arms that showed where their spots had been. These marks would take weeks to fade, Tiki knew. Even John Berra, the first to come down with the chicken pox, still had a few left over.

But it was Ronde's absence that was the real threat to the team. Thinking back, Tiki was able to count at least eight times this season where Ronde had been the difference between defeat and victory—including their last game. He was far and away their best defender—and Fredericksburg was bound to be the toughest team the Eagles had faced.

In the history of Hidden Valley, only one team had ever won a state championship, and that was way back in 1943! If they won tomorrow, they'd be the biggest celebrities in Roanoke! Tiki imagined a huge parade right through the heart of downtown, with the Eagles riding in convertibles, waving to their thousands of happy fans. . . .

Poor Ronde, he thought. He sure hoped his twin would be well enough to ride in the parade, if they had one. Funny—last week, *he'd* been the object of everybody's pity. How lucky he'd been that the Eagles had survived that game without him!

Would Ronde be as lucky?

The drive to Richmond took several hours, including a stop for lunch. When they finally got there, the buses drove them straight to the campus of Richmond University. They got off and were led to their rooms, which were usually used as dormitories for the college students who lived on campus. It was winter break for the college, so the dorms were empty. So was most of the campus, with only a few people walking around in the sunny, cold afternoon.

Their trip, their stay, their food and lodging, were all being paid for by the Virginia School Athletic Commission. Tiki couldn't help feeling like a VIP—a very important person. "Yeah, I could get used to this," he said, nodding and smiling.

After they'd unpacked their bags (Tiki was put in a room with Paco, his old buddy from Pee Wee League), the team walked over to the football field where tomorrow afternoon's game was to take place. This was where the University of Richmond football team played their home games.

"Whoa," Tiki said under his breath. There was room for thousands of people in these bleachers! One of the groundskeepers told him that the game was a sellout. All those stands would be packed with people, most of them rooting for Fredericksburg, which was much closer to Richmond than Roanoke was.

Tiki sure wished his mom had been able to make the trip. With her there, he knew the cheers for the Eagles would have been heard, no matter how many Falcon fans tried to drown her out.

They practiced lightly, and then Coach Wheeler gathered them on the sideline. "Okay, listen up. Fredericksburg is a real powerhouse, as we've already discussed. Best record in the state, tops in almost every category. Six-point favorites. Well, never mind all that. If we could beat the chicken pox to get this far, we can beat them, too!"

Everyone whooped and clapped, laughing.

"You all know your assignments, how we're going to approach the game," Wheeler went on. "I just want to address one other thing—the hype."

"The hype?" Paco repeated, not getting it.

"See those folks over in the stands? Those are reporters—newspapers, local radio and TV stations from here, and Roanoke, and everywhere else in the state. They're all dying to talk to you—so I wanted to make sure I got to you first.

"Whatever you do, don't say anything that could get back to the Falcons. No bragging, no guarantees of victory, no dissing the other team, no clues to our strategy— nothing but the usual 'blah-blah-blah.' Just tell them we're here to win, to give it our best against a great team, and to show our pride in Hidden Valley, and in Roanoke. Understood?"

They all said yes, though Tiki could tell some of them were excited. Not many of the Eagles had been interviewed before, and none of them had ever been on TV. This was going to be more attention than any of them had ever known.

"It's all about the game," Wheeler finished. "Just keep your focus on that. Everything else is unimportant. Got it?"

They got it, all right. But Tiki knew some of them would surely get carried away by all the—what was the word Coach had used? Oh, yeah—the *hype*.

Tiki wasn't worried about himself, though. He was much less excited than the others, and it was all because of Ronde. Nothing was the same without his twin, and Tiki found it hard to fully enjoy the moment.

Besides, how were the Eagles supposed to win without their best defensive player? Without the kid who ran back all their kickoffs and punts?

Wait a minute. Tiki had forgotten all about that part! Who was going to—?

At that very moment, Coach Wheeler approached him. "Tiki!"

"Yes, Coach?"

"Listen, I've been thinking about it, and I want you to run back all the kicks tomorrow."

"What?!" It was like he'd read Tiki's mind!

"Who better than you to step up and take your brother's place?"

"Well, what about Joey Gallagher—he did it once early in the season, didn't he?"

"Yes, but I don't think he's cut out for it. He's too big a target. I'd rather have a smaller, quicker guy with great moves give it a try. So what do you say?"

Tiki tried to say something, but his mouth was suddenly so dry he couldn't speak.

"Okay, then?" Wheeler asked.

Tiki nodded slowly. *I'm a dead man,* he thought.

When he'd foolishly promised his brother a victory, it hadn't occurred to Tiki that he'd have to be anything else than a running back.

What if he fumbled a kick? What if he lost the game for the Eagles by making a mistake while doing Ronde's job? *It would be the worst nightmare of his whole life!*

"Oh, and one more thing," Wheeler said. "The weather forecast for tomorrow is for rain all day. The field will probably be soaked, and slippery. So take care of the ball, all right? We can't afford to fumble it away."

Tiki nodded again, still unable to get a word out.

"Okay, then. Time for your close-up, Tiki." Wheeler waved to the TV reporters, who grabbed their cameras and hurried over to the Eagles to get their interviews.

Tiki didn't talk much with the press. Even after a drink of water, he still couldn't think of anything clever to say. He was too worried about tomorrow's game—more worried than any of his teammates. After all, he was the *only* one who'd be playing a position he'd never even practiced at. Besides, it was up to *him* to step up for his sick brother, and lead the team to victory.

That night, as Tiki went to bed, he wished for a miracle—because he was sure that's what it was going to take to save the Eagles.

CHAPTER TWELVE

A MIRACLE

RONDE SAT AT HIS BEDROOM DESK, HIS CHIN propped up by both hands, leaning on his elbows and staring out the window.

It was Saturday afternoon, 2:45. In fifteen minutes, Tiki and the rest of the Eagles would take the field for the game of their lives. They would win, or lose, without him. Ronde stared out at the cold, gray December day. Snowflakes were falling, but nothing was sticking to the ground. The day looked like he felt—miserable.

Downstairs, he heard his mom getting ready to go to work. She was making a lot of noise—putting his dinner in the fridge, complete with written instructions for him on how to prepare each dish. Today, like every Saturday, she would work from three to nine at her second job. She had told her boss she needed to take the day off to go to Richmond. But after Ronde got sick, she'd called back to say she'd be coming in after all.

If he hadn't come down with the stupid chicken pox, Ronde thought sadly, his mom would have been with him and Tiki in Richmond, taking two whole days off from work to be with her boys while they fought for the state championship.

Instead, she had to go to work, and he'd be alone in the house with his misery. He would tune the radio to the local news station, which was going to broadcast the game live from Richmond—that's how big this whole Eagle phenomenon had grown.

Ronde wished he could take a big giant eraser and scrub his face and body with it till all those stupid spots were gone. No matter how much it would hurt, he'd go ahead and do it, just so he could play in the game today.

He sighed, and sunk his chin deeper into his hands. What was he thinking? Even if he had a giant magical eraser, it wouldn't matter—it would be too late to get there anyway. Richmond was five hours away. By the time he arrived, the game would be over.

Unless, of course, he also had a *teleporter* to *beam* him to Richmond in an instant. Like they did on *Star Trek*. But of course, there was no such thing. Nor was there any magic chicken-pox eraser.

No, what Ronde needed wasn't any of those things. What he needed was a *miracle*. But there weren't very many of them in real life either, he knew.

There was a soft knock at his door. He hadn't noticed his mom come up the stairs, but there she was now, looking at him with a sorry expression on her face.

"I have to go," she said softly. "You going to be all right?"

Ronde sighed again. He just couldn't stop sighing for the life of him. "I'm okay."

"You going to listen to the game?" she asked, nodding toward the radio that was sitting on the desk next to him.

"I guess so . . . maybe not, though."

She came over and kissed his head. "You do whatever you want to, Ronde. It's a real shame you can't be there, and I know how badly you feel about it. But there'll be other games, believe me."

"Yeah, right," Ronde said, his frustration beginning to show. He knew she was probably right—but what if he never got to play in another championship game? He would have missed his one and only chance!

"Your spots look better. *Almost* good enough to play football. Too bad they didn't look that good yesterday."

He sighed for the thousandth time.

"I'm sorry. I shouldn't even have mentioned it. But you do look much better."

"Too late," he said.

"Well. I'll be back by nine-thirty. Dinner's—"

"I know, Ma," he told her, sounding slightly annoyed in spite of himself. He wasn't mad at her—he was mad at the world, and his own lousy luck.

"Well, bye-bye, baby," she said, kissing him on the head again. "I've got to go."

"Love you, Mom," he said, hugging her, and fighting the urge to burst into tears.

"Be strong, Ronde. There are worse things in life, believe me."

"I know it," he said, "but that doesn't make me feel any better."

"Of course not." She kissed him again, and left the room.

He sat there, listening as her footsteps went down the stairs and out the front door. It closed with a thud, and then the house was completely silent.

He sat there, drinking it in. The only sound was the splash of cars driving down the wet street. He looked at the clock. Almost three o'clock.

Ronde had to know. He had to. He reached out and turned on the radio.

". . . Instead, we'll be returning you to our usual broadcast, the *Saturday Financial Week in Review*."

"Huh?" What was going on? Had they decided not to broadcast the game? *Why?* He was sure more people were interested in the championship game than some dumb financial show!

". . . Again, the state championship game between our own Hidden Valley Eagles and the Fredericksburg Falcons has been postponed until tomorrow at eleven a.m., due to the ice storm that hit the Richmond area this morning. We'll be bringing it to you live, with pre-game starting at 10:30. . . ."

Ronde shot up out of his seat. "MOM!" he shouted. "MOM!"

He ran to the window and yanked it open, then stuck his head out and yelled to her as she backed out of the driveway in their old station wagon. "MOM! WAIT!!!"

She had finished backing out, and was about to pull away when she saw him leaning halfway out the window and hit the brakes. Pulling back into the driveway, she got out and yelled, "Ronde! What are you doing? Do you want to fall and break your neck? Get back inside!"

"MOM!" he yelled, his face breaking out into a gigantic smile. "The game was postponed till tomorrow! There was an ice storm in Richmond!"

"Oh, my goodness!" she said, realizing at once what he was getting at, and why he was grinning at her like a boy whose greatest wish has just come true. "Just a minute, I'm coming inside."

He flew down the stairs and met her in the living room. He was jumping up and down and his hands were flailing all around him. "Mom! It's a miracle! Now I can play in the game after all!"

"Just a minute now," she said, holding up a hand. "Calm down and let me think about this. . . ."

"Mom, you said I was all better—"

"I said you were MUCH better, not ALL better," she reminded him.

"By tomorrow I'll be totally over it!" he said, tugging at her coat.

"I don't know," she said. Then, seeing the pained look

on his face, she gave in. "Oh, well, I suppose it's worth the chance."

"Yesss!" he hissed, pumping a fist in triumph.

"You go pack yourself a bag while I phone my boss. And don't forget to pack a toothbrush! Ronde! Do you hear me?"

But he was already up the stairs and into his closet, dragging out the cardboard suitcase he still had from the time they'd gone to Washington, D.C., for a visit when he and Tiki were in fourth grade.

Downstairs, he heard his mom on the phone, and stopped what he was doing for a moment.

"Yes, I know I said I could come in after all," she was saying. "But things have changed, and I need to get to Richmond. . . . Yes, it is an emergency . . . . That's a private family matter, and I'd rather not go into it. . . . Well, I'm sorry if it's not convenient, but I'll be happy to make it up in overtime after the holidays. . . ."

Gee, thought Ronde. He sure hoped he wasn't getting his mom into trouble at work. He knew they needed every penny she made to pay the family's bills. She worked so hard, and took care of the two of them as well as any mom in the world. And now she was making her boss mad, and losing pay, just to take him to Richmond so he could play—*maybe*—in the big game.

Ronde swore to himself that as soon as he was old enough to get working papers, he'd get a job and turn over every penny he made to his mom. And if he ever achieved his greatest dream and made it to the NFL, he was going to treat her like the Queen of the Universe— because as far as he was concerned, that's what she was.

Mrs. Barber poked her head in the door. "There, that's done." Then she saw him staring at her. "What are you doing, standing there like a fool?" she asked. "We've got no time to waste, Ronde—we've got to get on the road if we're going to get to Richmond in time!"

CHAPTER THIRTEEN

THE GAME OF THEIR LIVES

THE MORNING OF THE GAME WAS WEIRD FROM the moment Tiki woke up. He had a heavy feeling in the pit of his stomach, and a weird sense of doom hung over him.

Paco didn't seem like his usual bubbly self either. When they went down for breakfast in the cafeteria with the rest of the team, it was unusually quiet. Nobody made any jokes, the way they usually did.

Yesterday, they'd been all revved up and ready to play, Ronde or no Ronde. After their interviews with the press, and their pre-game meeting with Coach Wheeler, the team had been as primed as they could be. And then, the ice storm had changed everything.

A whole, boring day had come and gone. It was too miserable to go outside, so they'd all stayed in their dorm rooms and watched TV. They'd gone to bed early, but to look at them now, it was clear that not many of the Eagles had slept well last night.

Coach Wheeler and his assistants came into the cafeteria and sat down with the rest of them. "Hey, hey," he said, noticing the unusual quiet. "What's this, a funeral or something? Come on, you guys, pep it up!"

Nobody did, though.

"Boy," said the Coach, "I hope you get more excited when it's game time."

"How's the field, Coach?" Cody asked.

"Good enough to play, they tell me. You guys ready?"

"Yeah . . ."

"What? I can't hear you!"

"YEAH!!"

"That's better," Wheeler said.

But Tiki thought it wasn't all that good. In fact, it was pretty weak, when you came right down to it. Not a great sign. He thought he knew what was really bothering the team—Ronde wasn't there with them.

Tiki wondered if they'd missed *him* as much last week, when *he'd* been the sick one. If they did, at least they'd gone out and given it everything they had. Now, it looked like the team had already spent its last ounce of energy—as if this last blow was just one too many. After all, he thought, how many setbacks can one team over-come in a season and still come out champions?

"Tiki," Coach Wheeler called, waving him over. "I want to talk to you a minute."

"Okay." The coach walked him to the other end of the room, where they could speak in private.

"You all right?" he asked Tiki.

133

"Sure," Tiki said, trying to sound convincing.

"Good. Because you know, you're the man today."

"Huh?"

"You're the one who's going to have to really step it up, if we're going to win."

"Me? Why me?"

"Because you're the best player we're gonna have out there today," said the coach. "And because Ronde's your brother. I know you're gonna win this one for him—and for us all." He clapped Tiki on the back. "Remember, on those kicks—just make sure you hold on to the ball. Whatever you do, no drops, okay?"

"Got it, Coach."

"Good. Let's go get 'em."

The day had brightened up, and the field, as promised, was playable. The bleachers were filled with over 8,000 fans! Tiki had never played in front of this many people. But that wasn't what scared him. It was lining up to receive the opening kick that had him so jumpy he couldn't stand still.

Coach Wheeler had laid out the game plan days ago. They were going to run Tiki at the Falcons all day long, until Fredericksburg brought their whole backfield up to help out. Only then would the Eagles take to the air.

On defense, they were just going to try and hold the fort. Hopefully, Tiki and the running game would eat up enough clock so that the Falcons didn't have the ball very often.

The Eagles won the toss, and Tiki trotted out onto the field to receive the opening kickoff. Standing there all alone, far from any of the other players, with 8,000 fans screaming, air horns blowing, and the tension mounting as the seconds ticked down before the start of the game, Tiki felt his legs getting wobbly.

His nerves were threatening to get the better of him. He gritted his teeth, forcing himself to concentrate, willing himself not to give in to his fear.

He was concentrating so hard that at first, he didn't notice the sudden commotion on the Eagles' sideline. The ref's whistle blew, but instead of the ball being snapped, the teams both broke formation and stared over at the Eagle bench.

There, the players were jumping up and down excitedly, as if they'd already scored a touchdown. But it wasn't seven points they'd added—it was a new player!

"RONDE!" Tiki yelled, sprinting over to his brother's side.

Ronde, grinning a mile wide and holding his helmet in his hands, was accepting hugs from all his teammates.

"What are you doing here?" Tiki asked him, amazed.

"The ice storm gave me an extra day to get better, and Mom drove me all the way here!"

"Mom's here too?"

"Uh-huh."

"Man! We can't lose!" Tiki said, hugging his twin fiercely. "That's my bro! Ronde to the rescue!"

"No, how about *Mom to the rescue*," Ronde corrected him.

All this time, Coach Wheeler had been busily explaining to the officials what had happened. The officials nodded, made a note in their scorebook, and informed the other team's coaches. Then they blew their whistles again, and it was time for the game to start.

As Ronde strapped on his helmet and ran out onto the field, the voice on the sound system announced, "Receiving the kick for the Eagles, number five—Ronde Barber—number five."

Tiki grinned and clapped his hands, jumping up and down with the excitement he'd been missing all morning. *Now* he was ready for the biggest game of their lives.

The kick went up, and Ronde grabbed it on the move. Stutter-stepping, he left two defenders grabbing air, and two others tripping over their own feet. Spinning, he left three more slamming into each other. Then, he turned on the burners, showing everyone in the stadium that no mere case of chicken pox was going to stop him, or the Eagles, on this great day.

When he crossed the goal line, he was holding the ball over his head. He never let go of it until he was safely back on the sideline, carried there by his teammates.

"Here, Tiki, hold this!" he said, handing it over. "I've gotta get back out there!"

Tiki shook his head in amazement. Ronde seemed totally better, as if he'd never even been sick! He looked ready to run right down the field again, without even stopping to catch his breath.

But of course, that was too much to hope for. Ronde suddenly kneeled down to catch his breath, and he wound up having to sit down for the first few plays of the Falcons drive. By the time he got back in the game, Fredericksburg was into the Eagles' red zone and driving. On his first play at corner, Ronde's man was able to beat him easily for a touchdown to tie the game.

"Tiki!" Coach Wheeler yelled over to him. "Get out there and handle the kickoff! Your brother needs a break."

Tiki was about to object, but he could see that it was true. Ronde was doubled over, his hands on his hips as he staggered back to the bench.

"Don't worry about it, bro," Tiki told him. "I've got this one."

He lined up to receive the kick, just as he had at the beginning of the game. But this time he wasn't nervous. He felt no fear. He was going to step up for his brother, come what might.

He grabbed the ball, making sure he had it tight in his arms. Then, he ran straight at the first defender to reach him. Just before they would have slammed into each other head-on, Tiki did a 360-spin at full speed. Before the defender knew what had happened, Tiki was five yards past him. Somehow, he kept his balance as he stumbled forward.

The defense finally caught up with him, but not till he'd reached the Falcon fourteen yard line. From there, he was able to run it into the end zone on the very next play!

"Now we've each got a TD," Ronde told him when Tiki got back to the bench. The twins hugged each other tightly.

"You're the best!" Tiki told him.

"No, man, *you* are!"

"Okay, okay, you win," Tiki said. "*I'm* the best."

"What?"

"Never mind." Tiki pushed him away playfully. "Let's go get us some more points!"

They were going to need them, for sure. The Falcon offense was hard to stop. By the end of the first quarter, they'd racked up twenty-one points. But the Eagles, led by Tiki, stayed one touchdown ahead, matching them score for score.

The second quarter was a different matter. Even though the field had been cleared of ice, the turf was still wet, and getting sloppier by the minute as the Eagles and the Falcons ground it up with their cleats.

Neither team was able to make much headway. Tiki

couldn't get enough traction to break any big runs. On the other side, Ronde kept slipping on punt returns and getting nowhere.

By halftime, the score was still 28–21, Eagles. But Tiki could tell Ronde was totally gassed. Coach Wheeler saw it too, and said, "Ronde, I'm sitting you down till the fourth quarter."

"No, Coach!" Ronde protested.

"Coach, he needs to play!" Tiki urged.

Wheeler shook his head. "They're scoring off us anyway. I'd rather have one great quarter of defense from you, Ronde, than two quarters of halfway effort. You shut them down at the end, and we've got this game in the bag."

The boys remained silent. They knew from the coach's tone of voice that he wasn't going to change his mind. And deep down, Tiki knew Wheeler was right. Ronde didn't have a full tank of gas to work with today. It was best to save him for crunch time.

But that meant Tiki would have to keep driving the ball until then. *Okay,* he thought, *it's on me to keep us ahead.*

"By the way," Coach Wheeler added, "I've got a little present for you."

"Me?" Tiki said.

"Me?" echoed Ronde.

"Well . . . I guess you can share them." He went to

his locker and brought out a shopping bag. Inside was a shoebox. Coach Wheeler opened it and took out a brand-new pair of extra-long cleats! "These should help you guys get some traction on that sloppy field."

"Look, they've got velcro instead of laces!" Tiki said.

"Easy on, easy off!" Coach said, smiling. "That's lucky, huh? Just make sure you switch them quickly, before the refs hit us with a delay-of-game penalty."

"You got it, Coach!" Tiki said.

"And thanks!" Ronde added.

"Hey!" Cody said, seeing what was up. "How come *I* don't get a pair of those?"

Coach Wheeler shrugged. "They had only one pair left in the store. End of the season sale, you know? But Cody—you win this game for us, and I'll buy new cleats for every kid on this team, how's that?"

Cody broke into a grin. "Deal!" he said, shaking Wheeler's hand. "Coach, that's gonna cost you!"

Fredericksburg got the ball first. Starting at their own twenty-three, the Falcons ran straight up the middle for a first down. Then they pulled an end-around, a reverse direction play that left the Eagle defenders slipping and sliding.

For the next six minutes, the Falcons kept to their ground game, smashing helmets all along the line, rushing for three yards here, four yards there. The drive ended with a play-fake—and a quick touchdown pass, thrown just high enough to avoid the outstretched hands of Mark Zolla.

Now the score was tied, and it stayed that way for a long time. Tiki was able to get good traction with his new cleats, but his blockers, with their usual footwear, weren't as lucky. They were being pushed around on the slick turf, and it was hard for Tiki to break any big gains.

The Eagles had to punt again, and this time, the Falcons ran it back a long way, getting the ball into Eagle territory as the third quarter ended.

"Okay, gimme those cleats," Ronde told Tiki. "Quick! I've got to get back out there!"

Tiki smiled. He could tell Ronde had recovered his energy. Good thing, too—the Eagles were going to need it!

The Falcons ran on first and second downs, gaining seven yards total. Then they went to the air. The ball went up, and so did both the receiver and Ronde. They came down with it together, and fell in a tumbling heap, rolling over and over and sliding forward until they came to a stop at the Eagle seven.

They struggled for a moment—but then Ronde leaped to his feet, holding the ball high and jumping up and down with excitement.

The receiver slammed his hand to the turf in frustration. Then he took off his helmet and flung it to the ground—and that drew an immediate fifteen-yard penalty from the refs for unsportsmanlike conduct!

"Here's your shoes back, bro," Ronde said as he reached the bench and took a seat. "Come on now, Tiki—if we get a lead here, we can hold it for the rest of the game."

"Oh, we're *gonna* get a lead," Tiki promised, fastening the shoes and snapping on his chin strap. "You just watch."

Because of the penalty, the Eagles started at their own twenty-two yard line. Cody began by throwing a twenty yard out pattern to Fred Soule. Fred caught it cleanly, but as he turned to run, the ball came loose! Three Falcon defenders leaped to grab it. Luckily, it bounced away from them and trickled out of bounds at the forty-five, with the Eagles still in possession.

"Okay, here we go," Cody told them in the huddle. "Southern Cal on two."

Southern Cal was their name for a short pass to Tiki. It started with a fake handoff, then Cody dropped back as if to go long. The Falcon linebackers dropped into deep coverage, and that's when Tiki slipped through the line of scrimmage, turning just in time to grab the pass.

Tucking the ball in securely, he headed toward the far sideline, meaning to break around the corner. He felt sure that with his great speed and his new, longer cleats, he could outrun anyone on the field.

He turned the corner, just out of reach of the Falcons'

speediest linebacker. Regaining his balance and staying in bounds, Tiki sped down the sideline, the roar of the crowd in his ears—or maybe it was the rush of his own blood pumping, he couldn't tell.

Finally, he was ridden out of bounds at the Fredericksburg five yard line—first and goal, Eagles!

For the next three downs, they tried and failed to dent the desperate Falcon red zone defense. Finally, on fourth down, they brought Adam Costa in for a chip shot field goal, and the Eagles took the lead, 31–28.

The Hidden Valley band struck up a victory march, and the cheerleaders danced and chanted. But Tiki knew they hadn't locked this game up yet. There were still four minutes to go, and Fredericksburg wanted this game every bit as much as they did.

Adam kicked off, and Tiki looked for Ronde to be first down the field. But no—this time he was trailing far behind, looking tired and drained.

Tiki shook his head, realizing that he'd forgotten all about Ronde having the chicken pox. He'd played so well, it hadn't occurred to Tiki this whole quarter that Ronde was still getting over a pretty bad virus.

The Falcons wound up with the ball on their own forty—great field position—and still with two time-outs left. The Eagle defenders kept yelling, urging one another on with every ounce of strength they had left.

Three yards. Five yards. Eleven yards and a first

down. The Falcons were on the march, and the entire Eagle defense was back on its heels. Worst of all, Ronde looked exhausted. Mercifully, before the Falcons could run another play, the clock wound down to two minutes, and the officials called time-out.

Coach Wheeler said, "Landzberg, get in there for Ronde!"

"But Coach!" Ronde protested. "I'm okay! Really!"

"I don't think so," Wheeler said, shaking his head. "Look, son, you've given it everything you had. Let somebody else pick you up now—it's just the last two minutes."

"But Coach—" Tiki started to say.

"Tiki, that's enough," Wheeler said, ending the discussion. "I know you love your brother, but he's out of gas. I'm sorry, boys. Hopefully, you'll thank me afterward."

Both Tiki and Ronde had to sit there, watching from the bench. They winced as Fredericksburg advanced, machine-like, on the ground, eating up the clock so that the Eagles wouldn't have a chance to come back if the Falcons scored a touchdown.

Five yards. Eight yards and another first down, with one minute left to play. The Falcons were already on the Eagle twenty-eight, and their fans were screaming at 1000 decibels. Now they threw downfield to Ronde's man—except now it was Justin Landzberg doing Ronde's job—at the fifteen yard line for another first down, smack in the Eagles' red zone.

"Man, he left him wide open!" Ronde complained.

"Cut him a break, Ronde," Tiki said gently. "He's only a seventh grader, and besides, he's not wearing those magic cleats. And give him his props—at least he kept the receiver in bounds."

Tiki was right. Because of Justin's heady play, the clock was still ticking down, and Fredericksburg had to spike the ball to stop time from running out.

There were only twenty-five seconds left. On the next play, the Falcons threw a quick sideline pass to the wideout, who stepped out of bounds at the four yard line. First and goal, and the Falcons still had nineteen seconds to play with!

On first down, the Falcons tried a lob pass to the corner of the end zone. Justin, surprised by his man's move, tripped over his own feet and fell to the ground! Tiki gasped out loud, and he wasn't alone.

Luckily, the receiver stumbled too, and the ball sailed harmlessly over his head. The entire Eagle bench heaved a huge sigh of relief.

Fourteen seconds to go now, with the clock stopped because of the incompletion. The Falcons still had one time-out left, but they were saving that in case they needed to kick a last-second, game-tying field goal.

Their only play in the meantime was to throw the ball into the end zone. That way, it was either a touchdown or a clock stoppage.

Suddenly, Coach Wheeler called time-out. Then he came over to Tiki and Ronde. "Ronde," he said, "You've had a little rest. Can you give me one or two more plays?"

"Sure thing, Coach!" Ronde hopped to his feet and started jumping up and down from sheer excitement. "Hey, kid," he told Justin as he came off the field, "nice job out there. Thanks for picking me up."

Tiki smiled and nodded. Ronde was being a good teammate—acting like a true champion. Now, if he could go out there and play like himself for a few more seconds, the championship would be theirs!

With the Eagle time-out over, play started again. On second down, the Falcons' quarterback dropped back, stopped, and fired a quick pass over the middle. He had a man open and waiting in the end zone—but good old Sam Scarfone got one of his beefy paws up in time to deflect it!

Third down now. The Eagles were only seven seconds from being state champions—but only four yards away from losing it all!

Tiki knew that if the Falcons didn't score on this play, they'd call time-out and kick the field goal. But they also had to make sure the play didn't eat up more than six seconds. To Tiki, that meant only one thing—a quick pass to the end zone, looking for their number one receiver—*Ronde's man.*

Sure enough, there it came. This time, Ronde was

waiting. He had dropped off his man, daring the quarterback to throw to him. Then he'd charged the receiver, ramming into him ferociously just as the ball arrived—and jarring it loose!

Now there were only two seconds left. The Falcons called their last time-out, and their kicking team came onto the field. If they nailed this easy, twenty-two-yard field goal, the game would be tied, and the two teams would go into sudden death overtime.

With Ronde already running on fumes, Tiki didn't want to think what would happen if Fredericksburg won the coin toss and got the ball first.

It wasn't a long field goal either. But on a day like this, with the field so slippery, no kick was a gimme. Tiki closed his eyes, but then opened them again—he had to see what happened!

The ball was snapped. The kick went up—and *hit the upright*! It bounced high in the air, and landed in front of the goalposts. *No good!*

The Eagles had done it! They were state champions!

Tiki screamed "YESSSS!!!" at the top of his lungs. He held his arms high and jumped up and down.

Suddenly, he was being lifted off the ground by a dozen strong arms. He was thrown from one teammate to another, all of them whooping and hollering and hugging one another like long-lost brothers.

Tiki finally found Ronde, and they grabbed each other,

dancing around and around in a circle until they fell to the ground, laughing and screaming.

Soon the whole team had gathered in a circle and were hopping up and down, yelling and holding their helmets high. The few Eagle fans swarmed onto the field to join their heroes. The team members hugged band members, cheerleaders, and one another, tears of joy streaming down their faces.

Tiki went back over to the sidelines to find his helmet, which had somehow gotten lost in all the commotion. By the time he found it, the Eagles and their fans were gathering in the far end zone, where the people in charge had set up a platform, and were getting ready to present the trophy.

Tiki was alone on the side of the field. Well, almost. Over on the twenty yard line, he saw the Fredericksburg kicker, kneeling on the ground, his helmet off, grabbing his head with both hands.

Tiki's heart went out to the poor kid. He'd missed a short field goal—one he probably would have made easily, except for the tremendous pressure and the slippery field—and he'd cost his team the championship.

Now none of the Falcons wanted to talk to him, or even look at him. They were far off on the other sideline. Some were crying. Some were hugging one another. Some were standing there dazed, staring at the crazy scene on the field, watching the Eagles celebrate a victory they were sure until the last second was going to be theirs.

"Hey, kid, you okay?" Tiki asked.

"Huh?" The kicker looked up, his face streaked with tears and dirt.

"That was a tough one, yo," Tiki said. "A lot of pressure. Don't blame yourself."

"Are you kidding? I lost us the game!"

"It wasn't just you. It's never just one guy. This is a team sport, man. One team wins, and the other team loses. It could have been us just as easily."

The boy nodded, then looked back down at the ground, still hurting.

Tiki put a hand on his shoulder. "Hey," he said, "what grade are you in?"

"Eighth."

"Well, look, you've still got next year. Keep your head up, and stay proud, and maybe we can do this whole thing again."

The kicker looked up at Tiki, then got slowly to his feet. "Thanks, man," he said, shaking Tiki's hand. "Thanks for that."

"Hey, I've messed up a few times myself. I cost us a game earlier this season."

"Wow," said the boy. "No kidding." He managed a small smile as he offered Tiki his hand to shake. "So . . . see you back here next year?"

"You got it," Tiki said, shaking his hand and smiling.

"And don't think we won't whup you again." He winked, and the boy laughed.

Then, with a wave, Tiki went off to join his teammates for the victory celebration of a lifetime!

CHAPTER FOURTEEN

CHAMPIONS

THE NEXT FORTY-EIGHT HOURS WERE A WHIRLWIND of happy celebrations, one following the other.

First, there was the on-field presentation of the trophy that crowned the Hidden Valley Eagles champions of the state of Virginia. The trophy had the state emblem on it, and the presenter (who was a real congressman!) told them that each of their names would be engraved on the side, so it could sit in the school's trophy case forever.

Then there was the locker room celebration, in which each boy got to hold the trophy and rub it for good luck. There were lots of hugs, and even a few tears from Coach Wheeler, who told them, "Never forget this day, you guys. For the rest of your lives—and even if it never happens to you again—you can always say, 'I was once a champion!'"

Then Cody said, "None of this would ever have happened without Coach Wheeler. I say he's the MVP."

Chants of "M-V-P!" and "Coach! Coach! Coach!" competed with each other, the noise bouncing off the tile walls of the locker room. Finally Coach Wheeler yelled for them to get showered and pack their bags, because they had a long ride home, and their fans were waiting to greet them at Hidden Valley Junior High.

Ronde shook his head in amazement. Early in the season, Cody and Coach had had their problems with each other, to say the least. It was crazy how much things had changed.

The bus ride flew by. The team members joked and laughed with one another all the way, singing stupid songs, and reminding each other of crazy moments during the season—moments that were funny now, but at the time they'd happened, were anything but.

Riding behind them was a caravan of parents in cars—first among them, Geraldine Barber.

Back at school, just as promised, a large crowd of kids, teachers, parents, and neighbors waited for them. It was cold but the sun was out, even if it was getting low in the western sky. Dr. Anand told them that she had scheduled a big pep rally for the next evening—after the last day of school, and just before the winter break.

It seemed the celebrations weren't over yet!

The next morning's *Roanoke Reporter* was on the table when Tiki and Ronde came down to breakfast. "I figured it might have something you boys would want to read," their mom told them as she served them hot bowls of oatmeal with maple syrup. "So I brought it in for you to look at."

Right on the front page, the biggest headline was EAGLES FLY HIGH!, and under that, STATE CHAMPIONSHIP FOR HIDDEN VALLEY JUNIOR HIGH!

The article recapped their whole season, with all its many twists and turns. It was so long, the boys had to turn to an inside page to read the rest. And right in the middle of that page was a photo of the two of them, from way back in Pee Wee League, wearing their purple Viking uniforms!

"Hey!" Tiki cried out. "What in the—?"

"Mom!" Ronde shouted. "Where'd they get this dumb old picture?"

She laughed, wagging her finger. "I wasn't going to let my boys hide their light under a bushel—and neither should you! Everything you achieved on the team this year, you earned the hard way. And that goes for all the Eagles! You really played proud, and you should be even prouder now."

"Okay," Ronde said, "but couldn't you find a more recent picture? This one makes us look like we're in kindergarten."

She shrugged. "Sorry—it was the first one I found. There wasn't a lot of time to go looking. Just make sure you get some good pictures taken at the pep rally tonight."

The pep rally began with the band playing the Hidden Valley victory march. Then Dr. Anand stepped up to the podium, and made a speech about the Eagles' incredible season.

Afterward, she invited first Coach Wheeler to speak. He went over a lot of the same stuff—how he'd stepped in just at the start of the season, how he'd had to win over the team, and convince them that watching video of themselves and their opponents was worthwhile, how proud he was of each of his Eagles, and how much he had enjoyed the challenge.

Listening to him, Ronde wondered if Coach Wheeler would be back next season. It was possible, he realized, that Coach Spangler would return from his temporary job at the high school.

Ronde felt torn—Coach Spangler was known as one of the best coaches in the state, at any level. On the other hand, he loved playing for Coach Wheeler, and they'd won a state title together.

"Now," Wheeler went on, "I'd like to honor all our players who will be moving on to high school next year— they've been fantastic, and we're all going to miss them, but we know they're going on to bigger and better things. So, please stand up—Sam Scarfone . . . Cody Hansen . . . Fred Soule . . . Joe Gallagher . . . John Berra . . ." Applause filled the hall as each player got up and waved.

As the coach went on and on, Ronde realized with alarm that next year, their team would be much differ- ent—and much younger and less experienced. He and

Tiki would be the true leaders of the team, and it would be up to them to set the example, if the Eagles hoped to repeat what was already being called their "Miracle Season."

The ninth graders got a huge final standing ovation, followed by a quick salute from the band. Then Coach Wheeler spoke again.

"Now I want to talk a little about the future," he said. "I believe it's a bright one, in spite of all these great players we'll be losing. I have faith in next year's team, because I know there'll be a lot of good talent arriving—but more than that, we have a great crop of kids returning. Adam Costa, Paco Rivera, Manny Alvaro . . ."

He named ten or twelve others, and then said, "In particular, we've got our two MVPs coming back—Tiki and Ronde Barber!" With that, and as the audience roared, he motioned for Tiki and Ronde to come up and join him at the podium.

Ronde got up, feeling embarrassed and awkward. He'd always been shy, but lately, he'd been getting over it some. Still, this moment, being honored as the MVP along with Tiki, was almost too much attention for him to take.

"Come on, yo!" Tiki said, grabbing him by the elbow and dragging him along, down the bleacher steps and up to the podium.

As they got there, Coach Wheeler brought two trophies

out from behind the podium and handed them to the twins. "Congratulations, guys," he said, shaking each of their hands. "You deserve these, big-time. Right, team?"

The whole bench full of Eagles, along with every other person in the gym, got to their feet, stomped on the wooden bleachers, and chanted "Bar-ber! Bar-ber! Bar-ber!" until Coach Wheeler quieted them down again.

"These two guys have, between them, put the rest of us on their backs and carried us all the way home. I am so proud, not only of how they played, but of how they carried themselves all season. How they helped the team play as a unit, not as a bunch of quarreling kids. How they helped a teammate who needed help as much as the team needed him . . ."

Ronde knew Coach was talking about Adam, and his difficulties staying on the team because he was failing courses. He and Tiki had tutored Adam until he passed his tests and was allowed to play again.

"And finally, how they helped me to stick with a job that, in the beginning, I thought I might not be up to. So thank you, boys. Would you like to say a few words?"

He could not have said anything more horrifying. Ronde shrank back, his eyes going wide. The last thing in the world he wanted to do was say a few words!

"Not me, not me, please, not me," Ronde said under his breath. He hated to be the focus of a whole crowd of people—unless he was playing football, of course.

"Which one of you wants to go first?" he asked them.

Tiki and Ronde looked at each other. Neither one of them wanted to speak, but the crowd was chanting their names, and wasn't going to stop until they both said something.

"You go first," Ronde said, giving Tiki a little shove.

"Me?"

"I'm more shy than you!"

"Are not!"

"Am too, and you know it, so just get up there!"

Tiki was about to argue further, but he knew Ronde was right.

"Okay, but you've gotta say something too."

"I will! Just go!"

Tiki shot Ronde a put-upon look, then stepped up to the microphone. "I want to thank all my teammates and coaches," he began. "We had a great team this year, and we did what we had to do to win." That got a big cheer.

"I really learned a lot this season, and not just about football," Tiki continued. "I learned what it takes to win, and to succeed. But I also learned that sometimes, you *don't* win. Sometimes you fall short. And sometimes, of all the people on your team, it's your fault more than anyone's. I learned that when that happens, you've got to pick yourself back up and play prouder than ever."

He paused. As he did, Ronde looked across the gym to

where their mom was sitting. She was weeping, dabbing at her eyes with a handkerchief.

"Aw, Mom," Ronde said under his breath, shaking his head with affection.

"There was this kid in the last game," Tiki said to the suddenly hushed crowd. "He was the other team's kicker, and he missed the kick that would have tied the game. They lost, and that was the end of their season, and he felt like—well, you can just imagine. But I told him to keep on going, to keep his head up—because I'd been there too, and well, look where I am today! Look where we *all* are today!"

That was it—the room totally exploded in cheers, tears, and hugs all around. Ronde thought for a moment that everyone would forget he was also supposed to speak—but no such luck. Soon, they were chanting "Ron-de! Ron-de!" and Tiki was shoving him toward the mike.

Ronde cleared his throat, and the room settled down. "I just want to say—" His voice broke—it had started doing that a lot lately—and the whole room cracked up. At first, Ronde wanted to sink into the ground. But after a minute, he realized they were laughing *with* him, not *at* him. So he continued.

"We had a great year this year. All of us. And we did it for all of *you* guys—for Hidden Valley Junior High!"

The room broke out in a big cheer, and Ronde couldn't

help grinning. *Hey*, he thought, *maybe this public speaking stuff isn't so bad after all!*

With the crowd only half quiet, he finished his short but stirring speech: "We had a great season, all right—but Hidden Valley, just wait till NEXT year! *You ain't seen nothing yet!*"

PLAYBOOK

SOME KEY AND COMMONLY USED FOOTBALL PLAYS.

STANDARD OFFENSE/DEFENSE

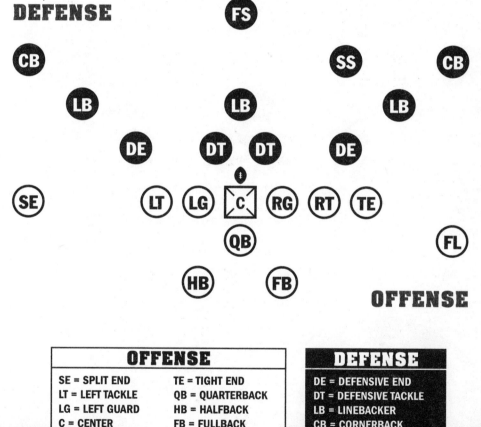

DEFENSE

OFFENSE

OFFENSE	
SE = SPLIT END	TE = TIGHT END
LT = LEFT TACKLE	QB = QUARTERBACK
LG = LEFT GUARD	HB = HALFBACK
C = CENTER	FB = FULLBACK
RG = RIGHT GUARD	FL = FLANKER
RT = RIGHT TACKLE	

DEFENSE
DE = DEFENSIVE END
DT = DEFENSIVE TACKLE
LB = LINEBACKER
CB = CORNERBACK
SS = STRONG SAFETY
FS = FREE SAFETY

OFFENSIVE PLAYS

SWEEP

THE QUARTERBACK HANDS OFF AND OR PITCHES THE BALL TO THE HALFBACK WHO FOLLOWS THE LEAD BLOCK OF THE FULLBACK AROUND THE TIGHT END.

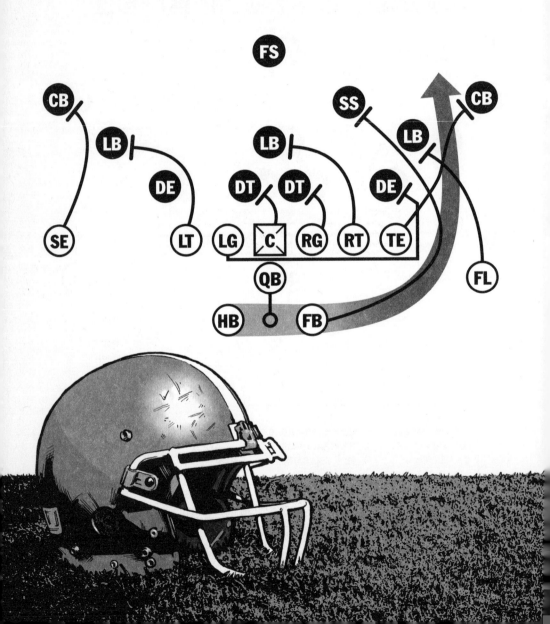

POST PATTERN

A PASS FROM THE QUARTERBACK TO THE SPLIT END. THE HALF-
BACK SITS IN THE FLAT TO DRAW THE LINEBACKER UP, WHICH
CREATES THE SPACE FOR THE SPLIT END TO CUT IN FRONT
OF THE CORNERBACK. THE QUARTERBACK DROPS BACK AND
THROWS THE BALL IN THE SEAM BETWEEN THE FREE SAFETY AND
THE CORNERBACK.

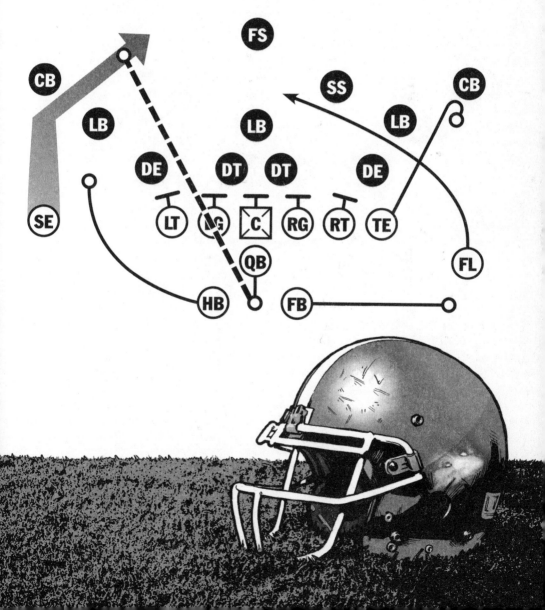

LINE PLUNGE

THE QUARTERBACK GIVES A STRAIGHT HANDOFF TO THE HALFBACK WITH THE FULLBACK PROVIDING THE LEAD BLOCK. THE PLAY GOES STRAIGHT UP THE MIDDLE OF THE LINE. GENERALLY UTILIZED ON SHORT YARDAGE SITUATIONS.

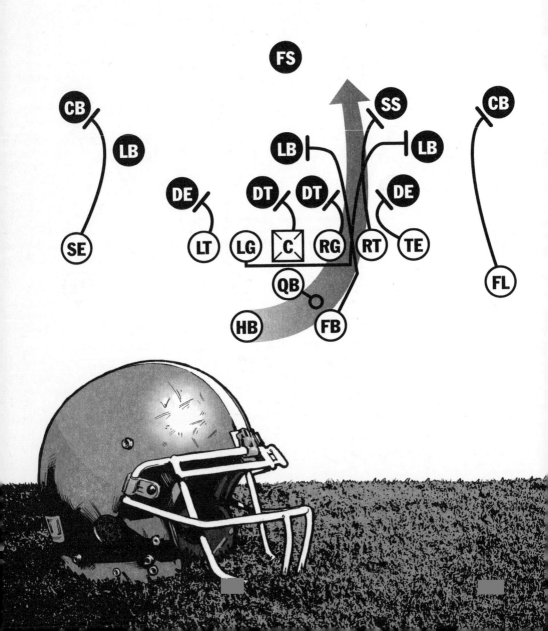

DEFENSIVE PLAYS

BLITZ

GENERALLY WHEN A LINEBACKER AND/OR SAFETY PROVIDES EXTRA ATTACKERS TO RUSH THE QUARTERBACK.

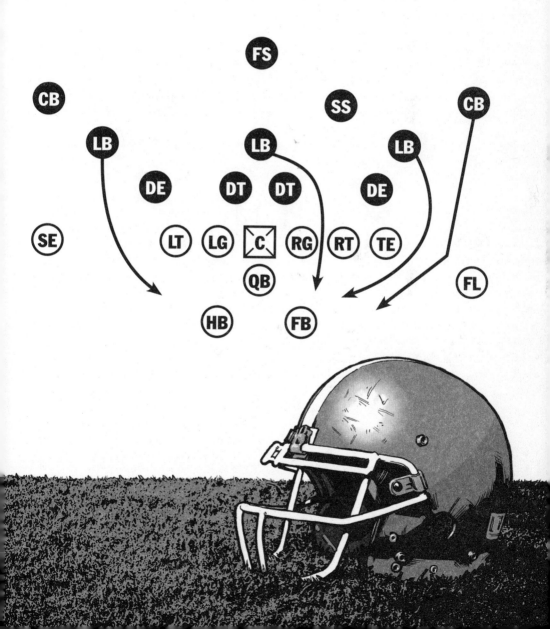

STUNT

GENERALLY WHEN AN INTERIOR DEFENSIVE LINEMAN SLIDES TO THE OUTSIDE OF THE DEFENSIVE END TO RUSH THE QUARTERBACK.

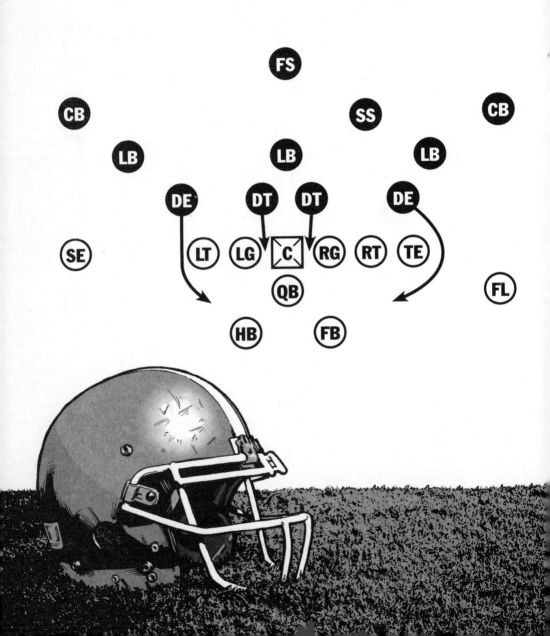

COVER TWO

A ZONE TYPE DEFENSE FOR PASS COVERAGE PURPOSED, MEANING COVERING A SPECIFIC AREA OF THE FIELD RATHER THAN MAN-TO-MAN COVERAGE. THE SAFETY GENERALLY HELPS THE CORNERBACK IN THIS PLAY.

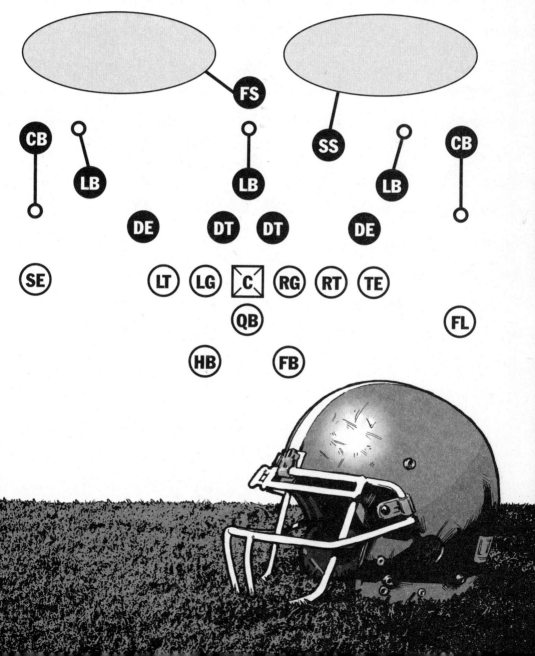